"I must go now, the princess may need me."

Kathy's voice trailed away as Leonid took a step toward her. "Please don't go," he said in a rather taut voice. "Not yet, Katherine."

"But I must...." Once again she broke off, for he had lightly taken hold of her wrist, and as a result she had begun to tremble uncontrollably. She *had* to get away from those suddenly limpid dark eyes that were devouring her face.

"Katherine," he said softly, "my beautiful little Katherine."

She ventured to glance up at him and saw that he was looking at her as if she mesmerized him.

"Your eyes are like the sky at midnight," he said. "Did you know, Katherine?"

And then his arms were around her and he was kissing her....

The Breadth of Heaven

by

ROSEMARY POLLOCK

Harlequin Books

TORONTO • LONDON • LOS ANGELES • AMSTERDAM
SYDNEY • HAMBURG • PARIS • STOCKHOLM • ATHENS • TOKYO

Original hardcover edition published in 1968
by Mills & Boon Limited

ISBN 0-373-01294-2

Harlequin edition published April 1969
Second printing August 1969
Third printing September 1972
Fourth printing June 1975
Fifth printing March 1977
Sixth printing August 1981

CHAPTER ONE

"WELL, that's that!" Miss Harbury closed her account books with a series of small thuds, and then proceeded to put them away in the capacious drawers hidden underneath the reception desk. She pushed a few errant strands of grey hair out of her eyes, and stared piercingly at the young woman who was about to take over her place behind the polished semicircular counter.

"You look," she commented abruptly, "as if you could do with a change. Don't you ever get out of this place? You've worked like a donkey ever since you've been here, and you didn't have to volunteer for extra duty tonight, you know. They'd have found someone—they always do."

The girl smiled slightly, and glanced around the softly lit emptiness of the foyer.

"I'm not very keen on going out," she said. "For one thing, I don't know many people in London. And I love sitting here, watching people—and talking to them."

"Well, dear, if my contact with humanity were limited to the chats I have while I'm sitting *here* I should think I might as well be in solitary confinement. But of course"—a small twinkle replacing the cynicism in the older woman's eyes—"I'm not twenty years of age, and even when I was I hadn't got chestnut hair and big blue eyes, so perhaps I don't know what I'm talking about." She gathered up her handbag, a library book, and one or two other personal belongings, and prepared to depart. "Well, I don't think you'll have many interruptions this evening—unless, of course, you get an impersonal summons from Suite Number One—so if you're quite sure you'll be all right, my dear . . ."

"Quite sure." Kathy, who had already started work, smiled up at her and patted her arm. "Go and have a really gay evening, and tell me all about it tomorrow."

When Miss Harbury had gone the foyer seemed quieter still, and Kathy sat back in her chair and closed her eyes. Although it was perfectly true that she liked the hotel when it was busy, and its elegantly clad guests moved backwards and forwards in front of her like extras from some particularly colourful Hollywood musical, it was also true that she liked it in its quieter moments, when the deep carpets and the solid walls combined to deaden any slight sounds that might have reached her from far off in the tall building, and the warm hush became a thing that was almost tangible. This was one of those quieter times, for dinner was over, and most of the people who were staying in the hotel at the moment—and there were not very many of them—had gone out for the evening. They would not begin to come in again until about eleven o'clock, and until then things should be fairly peaceful. She had always found it pleasant to be on duty in the evenings, and although this particular night should have been her own night off, and another girl should have been in charge of the desk, when the other girl developed a very nasty form of bronchitis she had quite willingly volunteered to take her place.

Ransome's was a luxury hotel—but as luxury hotels go it was a small and unostentatious one, and undoubtedly its somewhat exalted clientele were attracted mainly by its secluded dignity, its air of slightly old-fashioned respectability, and above all by the unquestionable discretion of its staff. The name of Ransome's was famous throughout the world, and undoubtedly many of its patrons came to seek shelter behind its sober Georgian façade because their parents, and in some cases even their grandparents, had done so before them.

Kathy opened the register, and cast her eye down the list of people who had booked themselves in during the twenty-four hours since she had last been on duty. There was an Italian countess, the Contessa di Lina—probably in London for the Christmas shopping. And there was Doctor Andrew Harding, an eminent specialist from the north of England who always stayed at Ransome's when he came south to attend a medical gathering of any kind. Then there was a rather large Spanish family who had apparently stayed for one night only. Apart from these there were no new arrivals, and the hotel, it seemed, was at the moment very nearly empty—or would have been had it not been for the occupant of Suite Number One, and the various persons accompanying her.

A telephone shrilled at Kathy's elbow, and she swiftly lifted the receiver, her other hand closing the register and pushing it aside.

"Reception . . . can I help you?"

"Who is that, please?" The voice at the other end of the line was feminine and extremely attractive, with a pronounced alien accent. It had become familiar to most members of the hotel staff during the last few days, and recognising it, Kathy felt slightly nervous.

"This is reception, madam. What can I do for you?"

"But *who* is it?"

"It's Katherine Grant, madam. Miss Wentworth should have been on duty tonight, but—"

"It is the one with the red hair, yes? Please, Miss Grant, will you come up to see me? It is . . . terribly important!"

For the first time, Kathy realized that the voice at the other end sounded violently agitated, and she wondered whether she ought to transfer the call to the manager's office. When Her Serene Highness Princess Natalia of Tirhania was agitated, it might be a trifle risky for a junior receptionist to take on the task of soothing her personally.

She hesitated. "If you will wait just a moment, madam—"

"But you will come quickly, please?"

"Well, I—I think perhaps if you were to speak to the manager . . ."

"But I do not wish to speak to the manager. I do not want you to tell anyone about this."

"I couldn't leave my desk . . ."

"But you must leave your desk! This is Natalia Karanska!" with a touch of unmistakable hauteur.

"Yes, Your Highness, I—I thought it was. But if you would only speak to the manager—"

"I will not speak to your manager. Oh, please *come*!" There was an almost despairing note in the voice this time, and Kathy thought swiftly. It was so quiet—nobody would miss her. It would only be for a few minutes, and in any case, surely if she explained the circumstances . . . She didn't want to lose her job, but there had been something about the Princess's tone that had come oddly close to being pitiable, how-ever fantastic that might seem. She spoke quickly into the receiver.

"Very well, Your Highness, I'm coming up."

As she sped upwards in one of the hotel's three lifts, Kathy wondered what could possibly have occurred to throw their most important guest into such a state of agitation. And why, in any case, had she not asked her lady-in-waiting or some other member of her staff to telephone for her? She had arrived ten days ago, accompanied by her two children, and with them they had brought a lady-in-waiting, a secretary, two nannies, a personal maid, a detective and a chauffeur. Ransome's was not entirely unused to accommodating persons accompanied by a con-siderable entourage, but Her Serene Highness had nevertheless succeeded in presenting the management with something of a problem. To begin with, she had demanded that her presence in the building should be completely unknown to the outside world—an almost impossible request, since as the sister-in-law of one of the few reigning monarchs left to the world she was a much publicized young woman, and followed almost everywhere by reporters. The man-ager, Mr. McArthur, had been unable to promise her total secrecy, but he had succeeded in keeping the Press outside the hotel building. Whether this compromise had satisfied Her Highness no one knew, for she had scarcely left her suite since the night of her arrival, but at the weekend she was due to return home, and Mr. McArthur at least would heave a sigh of relief when he finally bowed her off the premises.

The Princess's suite, the finest in the hotel, was

situated close to the head of the main staircase, and it was not long before Kathy was tapping lightly on the outer door of the royal apartments, and wondering once again whether she really had been foolish in answering the imperious summons personally. She felt decidedly nervous, for although she had seen the Princess in the distance she had never actually come face to face with quite such an exalted personage before—Miss Wentworth had been on duty in the hall when the royal party arrived—and the thought crossed her mind that she was uncertain whether or not a curtsy would be in order. As it happened, however, she didn't have very much time to think, and certainly little opportunity for bothering about the niceties of protocol, for quite suddenly the door in front of her swung open, and she found herself very nearly pulled inside. Then the door was closed behind her, and an extraordinarily beautiful young woman was taking her by the arm and drawing her forward into the room.

"Miss Grant? It is so kind of you ... You understand, I am desperate."

Kathy stared at her. "You are . . . you are Princess Natalia?" She didn't really need to ask, for she had seen that face too often in newspaper photographs to be in any real doubt, and in any case she had once caught a quick glimpse of the princess. At the same time, however, she hadn't been prepared for quite such breathtaking loveliness. "I can't stay very long—" she began.

The Princess turned enormous brown eyes upon her. "But you will help me? You will, won't you? You see, I can trust someone like you, but . . . but . . ."

12

Feeling a little more confident, Kathy looked around her, and saw that there was nobody else in the room. What could have happened to the entourage? Why was she being treated to this personal and rather dramatic interview with such an extremely important person?

"Of course I will help you if I can, madam," she began hesitantly. "But I don't see—"

"Come with me, please." Natalia had darted across the gorgeously furnished sitting-room to a door that communicated with the next room, and she beckoned to Kathy to follow her. The other room was her bedroom, and even more lavishly equipped than the sitting-room, but it was very dimly lit, for only one small table-lamp was burning, and the shadowy folds of the heavy silk curtains which masked the tall windows lent it a faintly sinister atmosphere. Feeling distinctly puzzled, Kathy halted on the threshold . . . and then a sound caught her attention, and she saw what it was that the Princess was bending over in the dimness on the far side of the room. And as Natalia turned towards her with the child in her arms she moved impulsively forward.

"Oh, what a lovely little girl! Is she . . .?"

"She is my daughter. Her name is Nina." The soft voice trembled slightly. "She is sick, and I am so afraid . . ."

"But if she is sick you need a doctor." Impulsively, Kathy turned back towards the bright lights of the sitting-room. "Let me telephone—"

"No!"

"But . . ." Kathy stopped. "If she *is* sick . . . ?"

"Forgive me, but I am so frightened." This time it was the Princess who turned towards the sitting-

13

room, and as Kathy followed her she gestured to the English girl to sit down. The child was making small fretful noises and clinging to her mother, and when Kathy looked at her she noticed that she bore very little physical resemblance to the Princess.

"I have dismissed all my servants." Natalia's voice was matter-of-fact as she made this statement. She seemed a little calmer, and as she smoothed her ash-blonde hair her fingers were only slightly unsteady. "The Baroness Liczak, too . . . she has gone. And my secretary, and my detective." She spoke with a certain amount of satisfaction, as if she had attempted and successfully carried through an inordinately difficult task.

"But, Your Highness," ventured Kathy, "no member of your staff has left the hotel, and—"

Natalia shrugged. "Very likely they have not," she conceded. "But I—I have dismissed them. They were all my enemies, and I have rid myself of them." She paused, and looked down at the child in her lap. And then suddenly the pretty face puckered, and she started to weep hysterically.

"Your Highness!" Kathy started to her feet, feeling completely helpless. "Your Highness, if I can do anything . . . But I don't understand . . ."

"I beg your pardon." The royal tears ceased to flow almost as suddenly as they had begun, and Kathy was favoured with a watery smile. "I am truly sorry to behave so badly, but—but they have poisoned my little girl!"

"*Poisoned* her?" Kathy's eyes flew wide open, and her cheeks grew several shades paler. "But who . . . are you sure? We must get a doctor—and tell the manager! And the police . . ." She darted towards

14

the pale cream telephone which graced the writing-table, but once again the other woman's voice rang out to stop her.

"No, please! No one must know. That is, no one whom I am not absolutely certain I can trust."

The telephone receiver, already at Kathy's ear, was slowly permitted to fall back on to its rest. "Why—why not? I don't understand."

"No, of course you do not, Miss Grant. But listen to me—you see, I know what I have to do."

The little girl began to cry loudly, and Kathy walked back across the room and knelt down in front of the Princess.

"Let me look at her," she suggested gently. "I know something about first aid, and—and children's ailments. At one time I thought I wanted to be a nurse, and I had some training. Perhaps I can tell—it might not be anything . . ."

But Natalia shook her golden head slowly, and seemed to cling a little more tightly to the child.

"No, thank you. You are kind, but she must see a doctor. I would never forgive myself if—if she were not properly treated. But the doctor must be someone who is completely safe. Someone whom *you* know, Miss Grant."

Kathy thought desperately. "But I don't know any doctors in London," she objected. "There is a doctor whom the manager usually calls if anyone is ill here . . . but I don't know his name. I'd have to ask Mr. McArthur."

"That is of no use. Oh, please *think*! You must know a doctor who is near, and who would come."

"But I don't! At least . . ." A sudden thought occurred to her. Doctor Harding . . .

She spoke swiftly. "There is a doctor . . . a very well-known doctor. He is staying in the hotel. He has never attended me personally, of course, or anything like that, but I do know something about him . . . that is to say, he often stays here. He lives in the North of England, and he is quite important, I believe—he's supposed to be very clever. I'm quite sure he's absolutely . . . safe . . ." Her voice trailed away as she realized with a feeling of increased bewilderment that she still didn't know exactly what the Princess considered 'safe' and what she considered 'unsafe'.

Natalia looked as if she were trying to come to an agonizing decision.

"This doctor," she said anxiously, "he is English? And—and what do you say . . . respectable?"

Kathy felt an outrageous desire to laugh. "Why yes," she said, "I'm sure he's perfectly respectable."

"Then you will call him, please." As she spoke, she drew a quivering sigh of resignation, and stroked the dark hair back from her daughter's damp forehead. "We must take the risk."

"Well, I don't know—that is, I'm not certain that he's in. But I'll go and find out."

As she hurried along the silent corridors of the hotel, Kathy felt as if she might possibly be dreaming. When she left the Tirhanian Princess had been white with apprehension and crooning a little pathetically over her child; and she herself felt that her mind was numbed and bewildered by the Alice in Wonderland situation into which she had allowed herself to be drawn. She was still not at all sure whether or not she ought to contact the manager without delay, and put the whole problem in his

16

unquestionably capable hands. But when she thought of the appeal in the eyes of Natalia Karanska, and when she realized the extent of the confidence which that evidently rather nervous young woman was prepared to place in herself, she knew that she would have to go through with the thing precisely as the Princess wanted her to.

When she reached Doctor Harding's door she was slightly out of breath, for she had been hurrying and the royal suite was some distance away. She had really made up her mind that the doctor would almost certainly be out, and so it came as a considerable surprise to her when the door opened almost immediately in response to her light knock, and the doctor himself appeared on the threshold.

"Doctor," she said, swallowing rather hard, "can you come with me . . . to see a patient? I think you ought—I really think you ought to!"

CHAPTER TWO

DOCTOR HARDING was easier to persuade than Kathy had dared imagine he would be, and although he was clearly surprised and intrigued by the situation in Suite Number One his professional discretion soon asserted itself, and he approached the task of examining the small Princess Nina as coolly and matter-of-factly as if she had been a patient in any ordinary children's hospital.

She was an extremely attractive child . . . as Kathy had noticed earlier, quite unlike her mother, but no less strikingly beautiful, although in quite a different way. The Princess Natalia owed her looks to a pair of wonderful brown eyes and a cloud of soft pale hair, but her daughter's hair was black and shining, like sable silk, and her eyes were very nearly as dark. The only thing the two appeared really to have in common was the alabaster quality of their skin, and this, it seemed fairly certain, must have been passed on from mother to child.

Dr. Harding spent about five minutes examining Nina, during which time the Princess Natalia remained seated a short distance away, her eyes staring thoughtfully into nothingness, and her elegantly manicured hands clasped tightly in her lap.

Then the doctor straightened himself, and picked the whimpering child up. He walked across the room, and returned her to her mother.

"An upset stomach," he said shortly. He looked thoughtfully at the slim young woman to whom he had surrendered his patient. "Has the little girl eaten anything unusual today, madame?" he enquired.

The brown eyes were moist. "It is as I told Miss Grant—she has been poisoned. Her nurse—but what will you do, Doctor Harding? She will be all right? You will tell me, please?"

"Madame, she will be perfectly all right." The doctor was not yet very old, but in the course of his highly successful career he had already acquired a considerable amount of experience. His words carried conviction, and he was skilled in the art of reassurrance. Natalia plainly relaxed a little, and she even achieved a small smile.

"You are most kind," she said. "I am grateful to you. If he were alive, my husband would be grateful to you, but . . ."

Her lower lip began to quiver again, and Kathy was afraid that they were about to be treated to another hysterical outburst, but the doctor was not paying a great deal of attention. He was frowning, and after a moment or two he said abruptly:

"You will forgive me, Princess, but this situation is, you will agree, rather strange. Do I understand you to say that you seriously suspect someone of having deliberately poisoned your daughter?"

"But yes, I know it, monsieur."

"She is not very ill, you know. She may have eaten something that didn't altogether agree with her, but a child's digestive system is quite easily upset. I'll give her some capsules, and within twenty-four hours she'll probably be fine. Not a very thorough attempt at poisoning, and in any case, surely no one—"

"You do not understand, monsieur." The Princess looked from the doctor to Kathy, and appeared to reach a decision. "I wish to tell you everything," she said. "You, Doctor Harding, and Miss Grant. You have been kind, and very useful to me, and I wish you to understand everything. But first I will put my Nina to bed, and you, monsieur, you will fetch the tablets, if you please. You have some with you?"

"As it happens, madame, yes, I have."

"But I must go back to my desk!" Horror-stricken, Kathy suddenly remembered that she had abandoned her post more than twenty minutes earlier. Telephones could be ringing unanswered, angry guests waiting in the hall to raise some point with her—to collect their keys, even. "I am sorry, Your Highness but I simply can't stay!"

"But you must! Miss Grant, you must stay! You cannot leave me. Monsieur—Doctor Harding, you will tell Miss Grant, please, that she cannot leave me?"

The doctor raised his eyebrows, and cast a faintly sympathetic look in Kathy's direction.

"Miss Grant is employed in this hotel," he observed gently. "If she stays too long up here when she should be on duty she could lose her job."

"Then she shall have another job . . . with me!"

"But, Your Highness . . ." Kathy stared at her. "I'm sure you don't . . . I mean . . ."

"You are sure I don't mean it? But I do mean it!" The slightly childish face took on a look which was almost happy, as if its owner had made up her mind that her bright new idea would make a very considerable contribution to the easing of her

20

troubles. "Today I lose my lady-in-waiting, my secretary, my children's nannies, my detective and my chauffeur, because I do not trust them. I am alone with my little boy, who is five, and my little girl, who is only three, and I am frightened, because, you see, I have so many enemies. And then I send for you, Miss Grant, and you are very kind. And you are English, and one can see quite plainly that you are not at all likely to be here to spy on me. So, if you please, you will take the job, and I will pay you a very high salary. You will be useful to me, I think, because you see I must have someone to write my letters for me."

Kathy was dumbfounded. At least half a dozen objections to the scheme occurred to her, but when she finally found her voice the only thing she could find to say was:

"I don't speak your language."

"It does not matter. You will learn, and in any case it really is not in the least important, because you see I am not going back to Tirhania. I shall never go back. I shall settle in England, and—"

"And will no doubt spend your days writing letters to *The Times* on the subject of the unhappy situation prevailing in your homeland. A charming plan, Natalia. I have every sympathy with you."

The Princess gasped, and like both the other adults in the room she swung round to face the man who had just silently pushed the door open and made his way, unannounced, into the room.

"Leonid!" She sounded completely flabbergasted, and her cheeks turned a shade paler. In a voice that was scarcely more than a whisper, she said: "I did not know . . . I did not think . . . that you were in London."

"I do not suppose you did, Natalia." Gravely, he gestured towards Kathy and the doctor. "May I be introduced to your friends?"

"You had no right to follow me here. Or to burst into my apartment in such a way. You are not my guardian, Leonid . . . I am a widow, and independent."

The stranger sighed, and inclined his head, as if in complete agreement. "You are perfectly right, my dear." He was quite a young man, Kathy noticed—perhaps not more than twenty-nine or thirty—but there was a profound weariness in his remote dark eyes, and his thin, aristocratic features wore a look of slight strain. "Nevertheless," he added, "I think you have not many friends in London, and I had anticipated some such situation as this. Not, of course," permitting his completely expressionless gaze to fall once again upon Kathy, "that I can pretend to understand this situation. When I entered, this lady, I believe, was protesting that she did not speak our language, and you were endeavouring to convince her that this fact did not matter in the least. Am I correct in supposing that you were offering her some form of employment?"

Kathy felt totally unable to speak, and Natalia looked rebellious. "If I wish to employ Miss Grant," she said, "you cannot prevent me."

"Naturally I cannot." The almost black eyes were wearier than ever. "Then this, I suppose, is Miss Grant." He accorded Kathy the merest trace of a continental bow. "And the gentleman . . .?"

"My name is Harding. I'm a medica' practitioner, and I was summoned by Her Highness for the purpose of examining her daughter." The doctor seemed to feel that it was high time he himself explained his presence, since nobody else seemed likely to do so, and this autocratic young man appeared to feel that it required an explanation. "And I don't think," he added, turning to the Princess, "that it will be necessary for me to stay any longer. I will have the capsules brought to you, madame. Two every hour for twenty-four hours, and I hope the little girl will feel better in the morning. Good-night, Madame. Good-night, Miss Grant."

He cast another half sympathetic glance in Kathy's direction, and then retreated from the room before the Princess had had very much of an opportunity to realize what he was doing, and by the time she came to herself sufficiently to dash to the door and call him to return, he was already out of sight and earshot. She came back into the sitting-room slowly, and when she had closed the door she leant against it. She had left Nina established on one of the deep, comfortable settees, and the child was beginning to cry again. Kathy, who felt decidedly in the way, and had been about to make good her own escape, impulsively moved across to soothe the little girl, and the stranger looked rather wryly from her to the young woman by the door.

"It seems," he observed, "that I have come at quite the wrong time, Natalia. Is my niece ill? And if so, why did you call in that Englishman? There are excellent doctors at the Embassy—"

"The Embassy!" The Princess's eyes flashed, and she swept across the room to confront him. "The

23

Embassy is full of spies and assassins—Anton's hirelings, who hate me and both my children, just as they hated Vasilli!"

"Be quiet, Natalia!" The words were almost hissed at her. "I sympathize, of course, with your reluctance to offend Miss Grant by conversing in her hearing in a language which she does not understand, but if you must speak in English I think you ought to refrain from discussing matters which are so essentially personal."

"There is nothing 'personal' about it." Natalia seemed to clench her small white teeth. "Everyone knows that—"

"*Chérie*, you are overwrought." He took a step towards her, and placed a lean, well-formed hand on her shoulder. "Where is the Baronin?"

"I . . . I dismissed her." The Princess's voice had suddenly grown small and very slightly apologetic.

"You dismissed the Baroness Liczak?" The man's black eyebrows shot upwards. "In what way has she offended you?"

"I . . . thought I couldn't trust her. I don't trust anyone. Oh, Leonid, I am so frightened, and so tired of being frightened!"

Her face crumpled, and she began to cry again. Rather surprisingly, the man whom she had addressed as Leonid took the child out of her arms and looked towards Kathy.

"If you would be kind enough to hold my niece for a moment, mademoiselle . . . ."

His dark eyes were coldly distant as he moved towards her, and when, feeling slightly hypnotized,

24

Kathy had taken the little girl from him, he turned back to Natalia.

"You should have a glass of brandy, *petite*," he said, and his voice was amazingly gentle. "It has all been too much, I think. I will ring—"

"No, no, please. I don't want any brandy, Leonid. And I don't want to see anyone—except you, and Miss Grant. Tell Miss Grant she has got to stay with me! I should feel so much safer!"

At this point Kathy decided that it was high time she intervened personally. "I'm very sorry, Your Highness, but I simply couldn't just abandon my job here and start working for you. I mean," she went on, swallowing in sudden nervousness as the mysterious Leonid turned very slowly to look at her, "I mean, I would have to give notice, and—and that sort of thing, and besides . . ."

"And besides, from all that you have gathered tonight of my sister-in-law and the situation in which she finds herself, you don't feel that the job would be either congenial or particularly safe?"

"Of course I didn't mean that. I—"

"I am certainly not blaming you, mademoiselle. Your feelings are perfectly reasonable, for a young woman of your type. The Princess Natalia, however, apparently feels that in you she has found something in the nature of a sister. As you see, she is quite distraught, and since I have—as you say in England —her best interests at heart, I can only say that I hope you will accept this rather generous offer of a position in her service. You are not, of course, the sort of person whom I myself would have choesn as a companion for her, but—"

"Leonid!" From the direction of the settee, a soft voice interrupted him. "You must not be rude to Miss Grant. She has been very kind to me. She—"

"Yes, yes, Natalia, I understand. Miss Grant, do you feel able to accept the position, or don't you? I assure you, you have no need to worry about your present employer. I myself will arrange matters with him. As to the question of salary . . ." His expression grew colder, and something like contempt appeared in his eyes. "As to the question of salary, which is no doubt of paramount importance with you, I think you will find that any remuneration offered to you by my sister-in-law could hardly be bettered. And," drily, "despite any impression you may have received this evening, my family's employees do still receive fairly punctual payment of their salaries."

"I . . . I don't know . . . ." Kathy hesitated, wondering what to say. She felt deeply sorry for the Princess, but her brother-in-law's arrogance and obvious contempt for what he clearly regarded as a very ordinary little English secretary had irritated her to such an extent that she felt her own rarely aroused temper struggling to get the upper hand. On the other hand, the job itself undeniably possessed enormous attractions—would certainly tempt any young woman who had never even dreamt that such an opportunity could come her way. And then there were the children . . . Nina and her brother, undoubtedly a pair of pathetic babies whose lives were at present dominated by an obviously neurotic mother—for whatever reasons Princess Natalia might have for her nervousness it was quite clear that she exaggerated the danger . . . at least a little.

Kathy looked down at Nina, whom she was still holding in her arms, and found that she had fallen fast asleep. Then she looked up again, and saw that across the room Princess Natalia was watching her with a look of desperate anxiety in her amazing golden-brown eyes. The man called Leonid produced an elegant gold cigarette-case, flicked it open, and held it towards the English girl.

"You will smoke, mademoiselle? A cigarette may help you to make up your mind."

This time his tone was careless and totally indifferent, and she knew that her eyes flashed resentfully as she shook her head.

"Thank you, I don't smoke, monsieur . . ." Her voice trailed away pointedly.

He made a small sound which could possibly have been apologetic.

"I beg your pardon. But as my sister-in-law neglected to make a formal introduction . . ." He glanced at Natalia, who for the first time looked faintly amused.

"Don't be absurd, Leonid. You could perfectly well have told Miss Grant who you were yourself. Did you expect me to present her formally? Miss Grant," turning to Kathy, "this is my brother-in-law, Prince Leonid of Tirhania. And it is quite clear," mutinously, "that he has been sent by my other brother-in-law, the King—"

"Natalia, that is definitely enough!" Prince Leonid's voice was once again as sharp and biting as the crack of a whip, and not for the first time in the course of the last twenty minutes Kathy was conscious of amazement at the speed with which his mood could change. Only a very short time ago his

27

manner towards his sister-in-law had been gentle and solicitous—almost affectionate; now, as he gazed towards her, his face looked coldly angry, and Natalia flushed painfully, and bit her lip.

Kathy felt a sudden rush of sympathy for her, and in that moment she reached a decision.

"Very well, if you really want to employ me, Your Highness . . ."

"You will work for me?" Instantly the Princess's expressive face lit.

Feeling suddenly shy, Kathy said: "It's very kind of you to offer me the job. I don't know that I'm really suitable, but I'm quite good at secretarial work, and"—glancing down at the sleeping Nina—"I'm very fond of children."

"Thank you, thank you! It is such a relief to me! I shall be able to talk to you . . . I am sure we shall get on so very well together. And now that I have dismissed all my staff I shall have to have someone!"

Throughout this interchange Prince Leonid had been standing by the flower-filled fireplace smoking a cigarette, his expression utterly unreadable. But as his sister-in-law's final remark caught his attention he looked up abruptly.

"You have dismissed *all* your staff, Natalia?"

"Yes, every one of them!" Natalia was obviously summoning all her courage. "They were spies!"

"Even the children's nursemaids? You have dismissed them?"

"Do not talk to me of those nursemaids!" Her voice ascended hysterically. "They tried to poison Nina!"

He looked frowningly at the child, and then at his sister-in-law.

28

"That is a serious accusation. The doctor—the Englishman whose services you engaged—he did not believe Antonina to be in any danger?"

"They made a mistake. They must have poisoned her food, but not enough. They—"

"And Joachim?" he asked sharply.

"He is quite all right. He is asleep."

"Then I imagine there is little basis for your suspicions. Where are these people now? Did you pay them before you dismissed them?"

She looked slightly conscience-stricken. "I—I asked the Baronin to pay them. They did ask whether they would have to leave this hotel immediately, and of course I said no, I would pay for them to stay on until they had found somewhere else to go."

"How extremely generous," he murmured. "Did you ask the Baronin to pay herself as well?"

Natalia flushed. "Well, she could do so. She has the right to sign cheques . . ."

Prince Leonid stubbed out his cigarette. "I will attend to her," he said briefly. "But first, mademoiselle," looking at Kathy, "I will speak to your employer. And you will come with me, if you please."

"Yes, of course." Instinctively, Kathy felt nervous at the prospect of facing her employer under such circumstances; but on the other hand, she knew quite well that Mr. McArthur would be extremely unlikely even to show slight displeasure in front of Prince Leonid.

As they made their way down in the lift she felt too shy to say anything, but just as they reached ground floor level the Prince suddenly spoke.

"You do realize, Miss Grant, that the Princess Natalia is a very neurotic young woman, and that you may occasionally find her unmitigated society a little . . . trying?"

"I don't think she's neurotic," said Kathy impulsively. "I think she's simply rather nervous—especially about her children. She may have good reason to mistrust all those people."

"I don't think you are in a position to judge," said Leonid coldly. "However, I am glad that you seem likely to regard her with sympathy. You must always remember that she is an important person, and that she has to be protected at all times. Her upbringing has not been such that she is able to, as you would say, fend for herself. She has very little understanding of the world, and is quite incapable of looking after her own interests. She has"—smiling urbanely—"none of the toughness of character which is such an advantage to young women like yourself."

Kathy felt definitely staggered, and only just succeeded in preventing herself from retorting that in sacking her entire staff on the spot Her Serene Highness had exhibited a good deal more toughness of character than she herself would ever be likely to muster.

All she said, however, was: "I'll do my best to protect Her Highness's interests."

"If you don't," said the Prince coolly, "you will answer for it. To me."

CHAPTER THREE

WHEN KATHY awoke the next morning she remembered immediately that her life had taken rather an extraordinary turn, but for several moments the details of what had happened completely eluded her, and when she did manage to recall the events of the previous evening they seemed to her so fantastic that for a moment or two she found herself half wondering whether she had dreamt it all. But it was real enough, as she soon realized . . . and then she glanced at her watch and saw with a stab of horror that she had overslept. The Prince wanted to see her at ten o'clock, and it was already half past nine.

It didn't normally take her very long to get dressed in the morning, but on this occasion she spent so much time making up her mind exactly what to wear that it was almost five minutes to ten before she was finally ready to vacate the sanctuary of her own room. As far as she had been able to gather, her new job would commence as from this morning, and she was slightly uncertain exactly what sort of dress she would be expected to wear while on duty. But eventually she discarded the idea of putting on one of the neat grey dresses which she usually wore behind the reception desk, and settled instead for a rather attractive woollen suit which she had bought herself only a fortnight earlier. It was the colour of autumn leaves, and almost exactly matched her hair, and she couldn't help appreciating what it did for her appearance as a whole. She felt decidedly nervous at the prospect of what might possibly lie in front of her, and the suit gave her morale a much-needed boost.

Just before ten o'clock she closed the door of her room behind her, and started to make her way along the winding corridors of Ransome's to the Prince's sitting-room. As she walked, she thought how little she really knew about the sort of life that was now going to be hers, and once she even found herself wondering whether the imperious young woman who had engaged her services might already have changed her mind. But she didn't honestly think that was likely. She recalled the scene in Mr. McArthur's office late the previous evening, when Prince Leonid had coolly informed the hotel manager that it was going to be necessary for him to forgo the services of Miss Grant. Kathy had felt dreadful about it, for as it was, Ransome's was short-staffed at the moment and she had certainly expected Mr. McArthur to make some small protest, or at least to level some reproaches at herself. But she had underestimated the lengths to which Mr. McArthur was prepared to go in order to please so vitally important a guest as Prince Leonid of Tirhania. She had felt like an inanimate object being handed to the Prince on a platter, and as it had been very late by that time, and she had had an extremely tiring evening, nothing in any case had made very much impression on her. She remembered making some sort of an apology to the manager, and it seemed to her that he had more or less said apologies were unnecessary. One of his receptionists had so impressed the Princess Natalia that she now wanted her for a personal attendant, and nothing could have been a greater compliment to himself or to Ransome's! The transaction had been completed, Prince Leonid had asked her to come to his sitting-room at ten o'clock the following morning, and she had retired somewhat dizzily to bed. In the cold light of morning she was, however, beginning to wonder whether she had possibly behaved in a slightly crazy manner, for she still had really no idea precisely what sort of job she was undertaking, and when she came to think of it the Princess's words and conduct on the previous evening, and the air of mystery surrounding the whole family had been anything but reassuring. She could only hope that Leonid intended to throw some light on the situation for her benefit. At any rate, she would have to let him know that she must be told more about the situation.

But when, in response to a command to 'enter,' she found herself in his sitting-room, all she could think of to say was a rather hesitant 'good morning.'

She looked very attractive in the russet-coloured suit, and her eyes were huge and slightly anxious, but if her appearance made any impression at all on the Prince the fact was certainly not noticeable. He was standing by one of the tall windows when she entered, and as he turned towards her she thought that something remarkably like disdain flickered across his face.

"Good morning, Miss Grant. You are very punctual."

From the way in which he spoke she could almost have supposed that he considered punctuality a fault, and she hesitated, uncertain what to say. Also, as on the previous evening, when she had been about to meet his sister-in-law, she wondered whether or not she ought to curtsy. But in this connection at least he was evidently able to read her thoughts, and made a small dismissing gesture.

"If you are wondering whether you ought to make some sort of genuflection when you come into my presence, mademoiselle, let me hasten to assure you that I dislike such displays of anachronistic humility very much indeed, and the same applies to my sister-in-law. Will you be seated?"

She complied, sinking down on to a brocade-covered sofa so deep that its cushions threatened to swallow her, but to her discomfiture the Prince himself proceeded to pace up and down the room.

"Miss Grant," he began after a short silence, "there are a number of things which must be explained to you. I did not feel that last night was the time to talk to you about them, especially as you were tired, and obviously feeling a little bewildered, but if you are to act as a companion to my sister-in-law you must know more about the circumstances in which she finds herself. Of course, she will tell you all about the situation as she sees it, but her view-point is not exactly reliable . . . in fact, it is quite irrational." At this point, he snapped open his gold cigarette-case, and absently extracted a cigarette. Apparently he remembered that Kathy herself did not smoke, for he did not attempt to offer her one, but instead lit his own, and paced thoughtfully to the window before speaking again.

"The Princess Natalia," he said slowly, "is the widow of Kaspar, my elder brother . . . one of my elder brothers. She was very young when they married—not quite seventeen, I believe—and despite everything that has happened to her since she has remained in many respects nothing but a child. She is

34

extremely devoted to her son and daughter, but her feeling for them sometimes bears a disturbing resemblance to a small girl's affection for her dolls. You understand me?"

Kathy felt uncomfortable. "I thought," she said hesitantly, "that her anxiety over the little girl—over your niece—was very real."

"Of course it was real. She is very easily frightened, and for the children she is terrified. Which brings me to what I was going to say. My eldest brother, as perhaps you know, is the King of Tirhania."

Kathy nodded. "King Anton?"

"That is correct. Well, unfortunately, Anton is not popular with everyone in my country. Like so many of us, he has his enemies. Soon, no doubt, we shall all be in exile." His voice was dry, and completely detached. "However, where Anton has failed, my brother Kaspar, while he was alive, seemed likely to succeed. For some reason our people became strongly attached to him. Anton knew it, everyone knew it." He shrugged. "There was no ill feeling . . . they were brothers, they did not wish to quarrel. And then, one year ago, Kaspar was killed in an air accident. It was quite an understandable accident—he always flew his own plane, he took risks, and one day he was just a bit too rash. However," staring thoughtfully out of the window, "nothing will convince my sister-in-law that he was not murdered on the instructions of Anton."

"But surely, if she is so childlike . . . a very trusting person . . . ?" ventured Kathy. "Surely she would not suspect King Anton of such a thing unless it seemed certain to be true?"

35

"Of her own accord she would suspect no one."
Violently, the Prince crushed out his cigarette in a
conveniently placed ash-tray, and swung away from
the window. "Her mind has been poisoned, and as
far as I can see, there is no antidote to the poison."
He looked bleakly at Kathy. "I only tell you all this
so that you shall completely understand the situation.
Her Highness will talk to you of dangers and con-
spiracies—of a plot, which certainly exists only in her
own imagination—to rid the world of herself and
both her children . . . presumably because she is the
widow, and they the heirs of Kaspar."

"I . . . see." Kathy remembered the melo-
dramatic scene she had found when she first went up
to the Princess's suite the night before. "Then that
is why she has dismissed all her servants? She thinks
they have all been bribed to spy on her and the
children?"

"I imagine so, mademoiselle." He looked at her
coldly, and she realized that he had found the task of
discussing his family's affairs with her extremely dis-
tasteful. He looked at his watch.

"And now," he said more briskly, "there are a
number of other matters to be settled. . . the exact
nature of your duties, and the size of the remuneration which is to be paid to you." He moved across to
a handsome walnut writing-desk, and sitting down
before it started writing something. "I think," he
said without looking up, "that it may seem a trifle
strange if my sister-in-law is known to have engaged
an English companion. Officially, you will be her
secretary. As to the question of salary . . ."

He named a figure which took Kathy's breath away. Feeling impelled to do so, she said shyly: "Isn't that rather high? I mean—"

"As an employee of the Princess Natalia, Miss Grant, you will have certain expenses. For one thing, your appearance will be of considerable importance." His eyes flickered over her in a peculiarly humiliating fashion, and feeling that he despised even the russet-coloured suit, which had certainly not been very expensive, she coloured brilliantly.

"I—I understand," she said quietly, and hoped that the interview would soon come to an end.

He stood up and walked towards her, holding something in his hand. "This," he said, "is a cheque for your first month's salary. I doubt whether there will be time for you to do any shopping in London—in fact," looking at his watch again, "there certainly will not be time. But we shall be stopping in Paris and Rome, and perhaps Her Highness will advise you on the choice of a wardrobe."

"Paris . . . ? Rome . . . ?" Kathy stared at him. "We're—we're leaving London?"

Halfway back to his desk, he turned to look at her. "But naturally. Surely you did not assume . . . the Princess's home is in Tirhania, and she is going back there. I am taking her back, and you will come with us. Unless, of course," disdainfully, "this changes things as far as you are concerned? You do not wish to go abroad, perhaps? You are a timid little English mouse, afraid to leave the security of your own island?"

"Of course not." She stood up, mustering all her dignity. "I hadn't thought . . . I mean, I didn't realize . . . But naturally Her Highness will be going home, and it makes no difference whatsoever to me. I have no living relatives, or ties of any sort, and I should very much like to go abroad."

"Well, that is good." To her astonishment, he smiled, and it was an extraordinarily attractive smile, revealing excellent white teeth. "And now, I have detained you long enough. We leave Heathrow Airport for Paris in just under two hours' time. It will be necessary for you and your luggage to be in the foyer by twenty minutes to twelve. You have just time to pack, and also to have a short talk with my sister-in-law." A thought struck him, and he frowned. "Have you a passport?"

She nodded. "I went to Switzerland once, when I was at school. I had to have one."

"Excellent. *Au revoir*, mademoiselle." He held the door open for her, and realizing that she was dismissed she murmured something that she hoped sounded suitable, and walked past him into the corridor. His door closed behind her, and for a moment, feeling a little dizzy with bewilderment, she stood quite still. Then she hurried back to her own room, and started packing feverishly.

Twenty minutes later she had finished, and when she had taken her two small suitcases out into the corridor she stood looking around her bedroom for the last time. She had only been at Ransome's for a little over six months, but already she had become attached to the place. She knew that her job there had been absolutely secure, and she had felt at home in the rambling Victorian building, with its comfortable if slightly outdated furnishings and its atmosphere of timeless tranquillity. Now she was going out into an unknown world which was distinctly frightening, and

38

she didn't even know what to expect of that world. All she knew was that the people who inhabited it were rather larger than life—either quellingly aloof or disturbingly neurotic—and that it was going to take her right away from everything she had ever been used to.

She sighed, and walked out of the room, resolutely closing the door behind her. Perhaps the prince had been right, and she was a 'timid little English mouse.'

Precisely at twenty to twelve she arrived in the foyer, a suitcase in either hand. She had had a short chat with the Princess, who to her astonishment had been calm and smiling, and was evidently looking forward to the halt in Paris with the excitement of a schoolgirl.

"It is almost six months," she said solemnly, "since I was in Paris. I have practically nothing in my wardrobe! You and I, we will go shopping in Paris, and we shall have a wonderful time!"

Then Kathy had been introduced to little Prince Joachim, the Princess's five-year-old son, who was actually, she learnt, the heir to his uncle's kingdom. She expected Natalia to show some sort of emotion or nervousness on the little boy's behalf when she talked about the future for which he was being educated, but this morning the Princess seemed to have cast her cares aside, and it was obvious that the close proximity of Prince Leonid, who seemed to give her a feeling of security, was partially responsible for this. On the previous evening she had been certain that her daughter was being poisoned; now, as she bounced Nina on her lap, she was prepared to dismiss

39

the whole thing as having been nothing more serious than a minor stomach upset.

Kathy could not help wondering whether, as a result of this change in their mistress's mood, Natalia's erstwhile servants might be re-engaged; and when she reached the foyer it became clear to her that this was exactly what had happened. One or two of the people who had assembled there were obviously in attendance on Prince Leonid; but it was quite clear that the majority belonged to Natalia's suite. They looked at her with curiosity, and feeling vaguely uncomfortable she moved across to talk to Miss Harbury, who was on duty at the reception desk, and immediately stood up and grasped one of Kathy's hands in both her own.

"My dear, I've just heard," she said in a hoarse whisper. "I couldn't be more happy for you!"

Thinking that such congratulations would have been more appropriate if she had just got engaged to be married, Kathy smiled wryly.

"Thank you," she said. "But I'm terribly nervous."

"Well, don't be. You'll never get such a chance again! Enjoy yourself, dear."

"I'll try to." Behind her the lift gates clashed noisily, and as she caught the sound of a sudden uprush of activity she turned to say a hurried goodbye to Miss Harbury, but even as she did so a voice spoke icily in her ear.

"Miss Grant, I believe you are on duty?"

With a start she turned, to find the Prince looking down at her disapprovingly, his cold black eyes snapping.

"I'm—I'm sorry, sir—Your Highness!"

"My sister-in-law seems to require your services, to which, incidentally she has a perfect right. May I suggest that in future you remain close to her?" Without giving her a chance to answer he turned and walked away.

Hurriedly, Miss Harbury squeezed her hand. "Never mind, dear—stick it out!" she whispered. "Goodbye."

"Goodbye, Miss Harbury." Her cheeks burning, Kathy hurried across the foyer to where Princess Natalia was waiting for her. She was aware that several pairs of dark Tirhanian eyes followed her with half sympathetic amusement, and the Princess, when she reached her, looked faintly apologetic.

"I am so sorry, you are embarrassed, yes?" she murmured. "It is Leonid. He has not any—what do you say? . . . tact! and I only wondered if you would like to hold Nina for me . . . she has the great liking for you, you see!"

Swallowing her discomfiture, Kathy picked the child up, and was rewarded with an entrancing smile which transfigured the small pale face.

She was introduced to two or three members of the suite, including a thin, bejewelled, elderly woman who was apparently the Baroness Liczak. None of them looked as if their dismissal of the night before had discomposed them very much, but after all, thought Kathy, they were very probably used to it. To herself they were courteous and very amiable, if a little withdrawn, and she found it absolutely impossible to tell what they thought of her sudden addition to the household.

And then the majority of the staff were being shepherded into taxis which were to take them to the airport ahead of their employers, and finally the moment arrived when Natalia herself, in response to some sort of signal, moved towards the doorway. Kathy had been told that she herself was to travel in the same car as the Princess, and so, still carrying Nina, she fell into line behind her.

At the door, Mr. McArthur bowed respectfully over Natalia's hand, and then shook Kathy's with an enthusiastic cordiality which embarrassed her. Outside, they turned down the steps to a waiting grey Bentley, while camera lights flashed all around them, and a voice shouted: "Look this way, Princess!" Once, a camera was pushed close to Nina's face, and instinctively Kathy put up a hand to protect the child. By the time they reached the shelter of the car she was shaking with fright, and as the commissionaire closed the door upon them, and they drew slowly away from the kerb, she gave a sigh of relief.

Joachim, who was ensconced between her and his mother, looked up at her, and his huge dark eyes expressed a kind of precocious amusement.

"Don't you like reporters, mademoiselle?" he asked conversationally, in excellent English, but before Kathy could say anything his mother turned to him, and ruffled his hair.

"Hush, _chéri_. You must not worry Miss Grant." She added something in a language that was unfamiliar to Kathy, and the little boy subsided, and even closed his eyes so that he appeared to be asleep.

Throughout the journey to the airport Natalia chattered more or less incessantly, and during their brief wait in the V.I.P. lounge she continued to talk. In Paris, she stated, they would have a wonderful time. Leonid was prepared to allow them two days there—she didn't appear to mind having her entire life organized by her brother-in-law—and they would simply wander from one *couture* establishment to another. And then in Rome, apparently, they would do very much the same thing, and the result would be that by the time they reached Tirhania they would both be superbly equipped. She seemed to think that her own wardrobe was quite as desperately in need of refurbishing as Kathy's could be, and looking at her full-length sable coat, and the elegant wool dress underneath it which had obviously been the work of a top couturier, the English girl was rather touched by her naïveté. She herself was still wearing the russet suit, together with a lightweight tweed coat which had already served her for three winters, and she couldn't have denied that the prospect of buying new clothes was exciting. But the Princess's almost feverish absorption with the subject seemed scarcely natural, and Kathy sensed that it was simply part of an effort to help herself forget the other things that preyed on her mind.

They did not see very much of Leonid, who had driven to the airport in a separate car, and it was not until they were about to mount the steps of the airliner that he rejoined them. Natalia smiled at him as if she were glad to have him beside her, and for the first time Kathy found herself wondering exactly what sort of bond existed between them. It seemed to her that the Prince did considerably more than was strictly necessary when it came to looking after his sister-in-law, and although Natalia had not appeared exactly pleased to see him when he first came into her sitting-room at Ransome's the night before, in general she certainly seemed happier when he was close to her.

It was a bitterly cold December day, and the sky over London Airport was grey and lowering. As Kathy climbed the gangway an icy wind struck her face, and for the first time it occurred to her that it really was very pleasant to be flying off to Paris, Rome . . . and Tirhania. Down on the tarmac a television camerman was desperately trying to film them, but now they were almost out of reach—at least for an hour or so.

In the warmth and quiet of the great aircraft Kathy sank gratefully into her seat beside the Princess, and felt excitement surging through her. She had never flown before, and she felt a little nervous, but a stewardess helped her to fasten her safety belt, and as the engines roared into life she forced herself to sit back and relax. Soon the airport buildings were racing past the windows, and everything seemed to be shuddering gently. They were leaving England—for Kathy it was the first time she had ever been out of her own country since that schoolgirl trip to Switzerland years ago and she couldn't resist craning her neck to see the last of the tarmac, and the houses, and the grey December landscape.

And then they were airborne, soaring into the leaden clouds over London, and she knew that what she had done was now irrevocable . . . there was no turning back.

CHAPTER FOUR

IT was early afternoon when they arrived in Paris, and the sombre rain-clouds which had hung over London brooded also over Orly. Kathy felt stiff, and Nina woke up crying and caught one of her fingers in her safety belt. When the doors were opened the atmosphere, if anything, was colder than it had been in London, and passengers buttoned their coats and pulled up their collars as they hurried down the gangway and across the tarmac to passport and Customs control.

As far as the royal party was concerned, all formalities were made miraculously smooth, and within less than ten minutes Kathy found herself once again sitting beside the Princess in a car—this time heading towards the centre of Paris, and the exclusive, internationally famous hotel at which suites had been reserved for them. Kathy felt a little tired, and as the weather in the French capital was hardly enticing she would gladly have spent the rest of the day indoors, savouring the delights of the luxurious rooms—a bedroom, a bathroom and a sitting-room—which had been assigned to her. But they hadn't so much time to spare in Paris that Natalia was prepared to waste an hour of it, and so after only a very brief rest the two young women set out to visit Her Highness's favourite couturier.

Despite her enormously increased salary the products of the foremost fashion houses of Paris were still naturally rather beyond Kathy's reach, and so she only sat and watched while the Princess chose dress after dress from the current collection of Marière, and the obsequious vendeuses bustled round them in droves, but as soon as Natalia had satisfied her own immediate requirements she turned to the English girl with a brilliant smile and suggested that they should now go on a tour of the shops.

"You wish the whole new wardrobe, yes?" she said, her magnolia-smooth cheeks glowing with pleasure. "Dresses and coats and suits . . . yes, and sports clothes, and hats and handbags, too, I think."

"I—I must only spend so much," Kathy began, remembering everything she had ever heard about Paris prices, and thinking that it would hardly do to be too extravagant with her first month's salary.

"Miss Grant, if you are to be my secretary you must be beautifully dressed, or you will be miserable. So many smart women . . ." She waved one slim hand in an expressive continental gesture. "And besides, you are so pretty—really quite lovely—and you have to make a splendid marriage!"

Kathy flushed, but Natalia didn't notice. "All women should have husbands," she said. Their car had started to move off down the Champs Elysées, and she seemed to be staring rather blindly through the window at the passing shops and cafés. "The world is very lonely and frightening if you have no one to protect you."

Realizing that she was now thinking mainly of her own position, the other girl felt an uprush of sympathy. "Surely," she said gently, "you have someone to protect you? Prince Leonid . . ."

"Yes. Yes, Leonid is very kind." Her whole face seemed to lighten, and she smiled at Kathy. "And you, you are very kind. I shall find you a charming

46

Tirhanian husband, and you will live close to the Schloss Zaarensbrucke, which is where I live, and you will be my best friend! And now here we are at the boutique of Madame Rémier, and you can choose some suits."

Madame Rémier, an elderly and impressive French-woman, was clearly delighted that anyone as influential as the Princess Natalia of Tirhania had seen fit to recommend her to a friend, and she was also extremely helpful. Having taken one look at Kathy she declared that mademoiselle's colour was obviously blue, and seating her clients in a magnificent powder-pink fitting-room produced model after model for the approval of the English girl. They were all so staggeringly perfect, and she was so completely bewildered, that she was hard put to it to say which she liked best, and she was grateful for Natalia's invaluable advice and guidance. With unerring skill and taste, the Princess helped her to select all the items which suited her best and would be most useful to her, and by the time they returned to the car she had become the slightly dazed possessor of three enchanting suits—one in misty blue wool, one in a heavy champagne-coloured silk, and one in a tweed so darkly blue that it matched almost exactly the deep wood-violet hue of her own rather striking eyes.

From Madame Rémier's they went on to an establishment which specialized in evening dresses, and Kathy stared in fascination as some of the loveliest gowns she had ever seen in her life were paraded for her inspection. The Princess, it seemed, would have liked her to purchase half the shop, but she insisted that she could not at the moment afford more than one evening dress, and eventually decided on a subtly spectacular creation in midnight-blue tulle, with a draped bodice and a spreading ankle-length skirt which seemed to float about her like an undulating haze. When she put it on and studied her own reflection in a looking-glass she was barely able to recognize herself, for it did such strangely breath-taking things to her skin and eyes that the young woman who had helped her into it permitted herself a small gasp of approval, and Natalia, standing behind her, clasped her hands together and gave vent to an exclamation in her native tongue.

"But you are entirely enchanting!" she said, tilting her head on one side. "Tonight we shall go to the theatre, and all the French gentlemen will stare at you." The big brown eyes twinkled. "And now we will go and do the rest of our shopping."

The rest of the afternoon, as far as Kathy was concerned, resembled a rather confused dream, and when, shortly before six o'clock, they finally arrived back at the hotel, all she could really be sure of was that in addition to the three suits and the evening dress she was now in possession of several attractive day dresses, a bewildering variety of shoes and other accessories, and a mountain of extremely glamorous lingerie. She was still vaguely certain that the total cost of her new wardrobe was considerably more than she could really afford, even now, and it worried her a little that in almost every case the garments had been placed temporarily, to Natalia's account. But when she ventured to protest the Princess rebuked her by saying that her secretary must dress well, and that she could repay the money gradually. When she still gave indications of being unhappy about the situation Natalia evinced slight but unmistakable signs of being surprised and just a little cross, and Kathy realized that to persevere with the question at the moment would simply look like arrogance.

In the foyer of the hotel the Baroness Liczak was awaiting them. She was not, as Kathy had already discovered, a particularly expansive person, and as the English girl came through the swing doors in the wake of their mutual employer she knew that the Baroness was watching her with cold disapproval in her light grey eyes.

She spoke to the Princess in their own tongue, and her voice was prim and remote. As she listened to her the smile faded on Natalia's lips, and with a consciousness of foreboding Kathy saw her push back her silver-blonde hair in the nervous gesture which meant that something had upset her.

She seemed to be asking questions, rapidly and disjointedly, and the Baroness answered in the same coldly respectful manner. Then Natalia turned to Kathy, and her face was small and forlorn.

"The Baroness says that Leonid—that the Prince has left. He has gone on to Tirhania ahead of us. There is something . . . something that he has to attend to." She stared absently at the two porters who were bringing Kathy's purchases in and stacking them in the lift. "I wish he had not gone," she said, and all the gaiety of the afternoon was banished from her face.

The Baroness stood by impassively, like an automaton awaiting instructions, and Kathy felt more than ever irritated by her. Several people were staring at them, for although they had not been pursued

49

in Paris as they had been in London, certainly there could be no one in the hotel who did not know the identity of the fair-haired young woman with the magnificent fur coat and the air of being rather lost.

"I think," said Kathy quietly, "that perhaps we ought to go upstairs."

"Yes . . . yes, of course."

They started to move towards the lift, and the Baroness Liczak moved with them. She was speaking again, and something she said seemed to upset the Princess, who stopped in her tracks and uttered an exclamation, followed by a protesting torrent of words. But the Baroness, as imperturbable as ever, seemed to pacify her fairly quickly, and she fell silent, though her mouth was set in resentful lines, and on the way upstairs she hardly spoke at all. At the outer door of the royal suite the Baroness left them, but Kathy was urged to accompany her employer inside, and when the door was closed behind them Natalia flung her coat over a little gilt-legged chair, and wandered over to the window. Outside a fine rain was falling, and the sound of hissing tyres came up very clearly from the brightly-lit street below. Kathy took the sable coat into the bedroom and put it away. Then she came back, and picked up the telephone.

"I think you ought to have something," she said. "Shall I order you a drink?"

"Yes, please." The voice was quiet, and suspiciously husky. "A gin and orange. And order something for yourself."

Kathy transmitted the order, asking for a sherry for herself, and then she put the receiver back on its rest and looked at the Princess's uninformative and resolutely turned back. Feeling a little uncomfortable, and also very slightly exasperated, she wondered what to do.

Quite inconsequentially, she said: "It's not a very nice night for the Prince's journey."

"No." Natalia turned, and walked towards her. "Kathy, I am frightened."

"Frightened?" Kathy stared at her. "Why, madame?"

"The Prince has appointed someone—a man from the Embassy—to escort us to Tirhania. Such a one could be dangerous . . . how can I trust him?"

"Well, surely, if the Prince himself—"

"The Prince trusts people, Kathy. I cannot do so." She started to move restlessly about the room, picking things up and putting them down again. Her drink arrived on a tiny silver salver, and was placed on a table. She took it and sipped at it, and then sank down limply on to a settee.

"The Prince told you why I am frightened, I think."

"Yes, madame."

"He thinks that I am wrong, that I have nothing to fear, but . . ."

"Perhaps there is nothing to fear," Kathy ventured gently.

"You do not know my brother-in-law." The small, pretty hands toyed nervously with the stem of the glass. "My brother-in-law Anton, I mean. He hates me, and he hates Joachim. Joachim is the heir, you understand."

"But surely," said Kathy practically, "His Majesty could marry, and provide himself with a son?"

"Anton is married. But they say—oh, I don't know if it is true—that the Queen will never have a child of her own."

"I see." Kathy tried another idea. "But, madame, you trust Prince Leonid, don't you? Surely, if he says there is nothing to fear, there is nothing?"

"Leonid is—what you say—very sweet. He does not see the danger which is beneath his own nose, I think."

Feeling definitely startled, and thinking that 'sweet' was the very last term which it would have occurred to her to use in connection with Leonid, Kathy abandoned the struggle to make Natalia see sense. And having abandoned it, she suddenly began to wonder whether there might after all be some truth in what the other woman believed.

"When shall we meet the gentleman from the Embassy?" she asked thoughtfully.

"We shall not meet him! I have made up my mind." Natalia finished her drink and stood up. "He is coming to wait upon me tonight, the Baroness said. But I will not be here, and you will not be here . . . and the children will not be here." Her eyes were shining, and she looked as pleased as a little girl who had just thought of a way round the difficulties in her homework. "We shall fly to Rome by ourselves, you and I and Joachim and Nina, and I shall send a cable to Leonid, telling him that he is to collect us there!"

"But . . ." Kathy's mind revolved in circles, and she stared at the Princess in blank amazement. "Madame, we would not even get seats . . . if you mean we are to fly to Rome tonight?"

"But of course it must be tonight," with mild impatience. "Of what use would it be to wait until tomorrow? And now, *cherie*, you will pick up the telephone, and you will make calls to all the airline offices. You will tell them that Princess Natalia Karanska wishes seats immediately on a night flight to Rome—seats for herself and her children, and for one other person. And you will tell them, of course, that it must be kept quite secret." Rather wistfully, she added: "It would be nice if I could travel *incognita*, but everyone knows me, you see."

Kathy, appalled by the plan, did her best to talk her employer out of it. The whole idea seemed to her more than a little crazy, and completely irresponsible, and she was quite certain that if Leonid knew of it he would be furious. And Leonid had asked her to look after Natalia.

But Natalia could, when she chose, be extremely obstinate, and on this occasion she was definitely not to be moved. She had made up her mind, and beneath the warmth and utterly genuine friendliness of her attitude towards the other girl, there was always an underlying hauteur. She was accustomed to being obeyed—she expected to be obeyed.

Kathy didn't have to spend very much time telephoning before she found an airline only too willing to accommodate the Princess. Four seats were available on a plane which was due to leave Le Bourget airport at seven-fifteen. It would arrive in Rome a little over three hours later. Would that suit Her Highness? It would. A few small formalities were gone into, and finally the thing was settled, and Kathy replaced the receiver.

Feverishly and secretly, they started to pack. Natalia gave the astonished nanny the night off, and let the remainder of her entourage know that she was resting, and did not wish to be disturbed until dinner time. The man from the Embassy, Colonel Zanin, was not expected to call until after dinner, and by seven o'clock they would be off the premises. They naturally decided to encumber themselves with the minimum of luggage—even the Princess with true heroism confining herself to one small white suitcase—and Kathy was obliged to leave most of her brand new wardrobe to be sent on by Natalia's staff. She then had the cases taken downstairs, telling the porter who took charge of them and placed them in a taxi that they constituted the baggage of a member of the royal suite who was leaving that night, ahead of the rest, and although she was certainly not accustomed to telling lies, or even to stretching the truth, she thought she did rather well. When the taxi had departed, she went upstairs again, and found Natalia and both her children ready to leave.

They looked a pathetic little family, with Nina yawning fretfully in her mother's arms, and Joachim being good and solemn and grown-up. And Kathy longed more than ever to stop them from doing this rash thing. But Natalia was impervious to argument or at least there was nothing Kathy could say that had the power to move her—and so they picked a moment when the hotel seemed very quiet, and then slipped quietly down in the lift and out through the swing doors into the cold and noisy street. Had they encountered a member of Natalia's staff, they would have said that they were going for a drive around

Paris—however strange it might have seemed to be taking two small children out at that time of night— but they met no one, and both women heaved sighs of relief as their feet touched the pavement, and they knew that they had crossed the biggest hurdle.

The Parish rush-hour was not yet over, however, and as they stood outside the hotel in the chilling, soaking December rain, Kathy experienced a sudden moment of panic in case they should be unable to get a taxi. But they were lucky, and had scarcely been waiting for more than thirty seconds when one drew into the kerb. A minute later they were on their way to the airport, and Natalia was smiling because everything, so far, had gone smoothly—it was going to be all right.

They drove along by the Seine. There were a thousand lights reflected in it, and Kathy thought how beautiful it was, and wished that she could have seen a little more of Paris. The bridges spanning the river were like something out of a fairytale, and she could see the floodlit outline of Notre Dame . . .

It was very cold in the taxi, but the children didn't seem to mind, and Kathy thought how very well behaved and amenable they both were. Nina was asleep on her own lap, but Joachim sat between her and his mother, his dark eyes wide open, staring through the windows at the lighted streets of Paris, never saying a word. She thought he was the most self-possessed child she had ever encountered, and wondered how fond he was of his mother, and whether he ever wondered at the crazy, unexpected things she did. Whether it occurred to him, for instance, to think it strange that they were now going to fly off in an aeroplane, without his nanny and, in fact, without any of the people, with the exception of his mother and Nina, who normally made up his life.

Once she felt in the darkness for his small, gloved hand, but as soon as she tried to take it in her own he snatched it away, and she wondered whether he disliked her . . . or whether he was simply a very independent small boy.

At the airport, formalities were got through quickly and simply. Natalia had an account with the airline which they were using, and everything was made as smooth as possible for them. Because the airport buildings at Le Bourget were rather small it was not possible for them to await the departure of their flight in a private room, but the public lounge was not crowded, and even Natalia had no qualms about being seen by the few people who were already assembled there. Air stewardesses smiled at the children as they walked across the room, and an elderly American gentleman in a far corner beamed benignly at the slightly sleepy Nina, who gurgled disarmingly back at him.

Their flight was announced, and for a few moments they were out on the tarmac in the chill, wet evening air. And then the warmth of the plane swallowed them up, and for the second time in one day Kathy prepared to fly from one capital to another.

CHAPTER FIVE

THERE weren't many passengers on board the aircraft, and the few there were seemed largely preoccupied with their own affairs. This was a relief to Kathy, if not to her employer as well, for during the flight from London the understandable curiosity of other passengers about the royal party had become rather embarrassing, and at one point Natalia had even been approached with a request for her autograph. But tonight they were quite undisturbed, and as the great silver-winged airliner roared into the black, starless sky and headed southwards towards the Italian frontier, both children fell easily and naturally asleep, and a few minutes later, rather to Kathy's surprise, their mother followed their example. When she was asleep she looked extremely young, and for a while Kathy sat watching her, wondering about her, and what her future would be like, whether there could be anything behind her fantastic fears and suspicions, or whether her own imagination was her worst enemy. And then she sat back and stared up at the dimly seen roof of the passenger cabin, and thought about Leonid, the Princess's brother-in-law. He seemed so hard, so impenetrably cold, and yet Natalia had said that he was very kind, and she herself had seen how suddenly his dark eyes could smile, lighting up their shadowy depths with a tremendous warmth. He had been cruelly, quite unnecessarily rude to her in the foyer at Ransome's, when she had been saying goodbye to Miss Harbury . . . But she had seen him smile, and it lingered in her memory. She hoped he would not be angry with her for letting the Princess leave Paris without her escort . . . she thought that if he were really angry it would probably be unbearable.

She was falling asleep now, and her eyelids were getting heavy, but in front of her she still seemed to see a pair of smiling eyes. She didn't want to do anything to stop them smiling . . . Very slowly they faded away, and then she was fast asleep.

When Kathy awoke it was nearly an hour later, just after a quarter past eight, and a stewardess was bending over her. She was speaking very softly, and Kathy realized that she didn't want to awaken the Princess, who was still slumbering peacefully, her pale hair falling in a shining cascade across her face.

"Miss Grant, we are to make an unexpected landing at Genoa. I do not know why . . . I expect there is some technical reason. There is nothing the matter with the aircraft, of course—nothing at all to worry about. Will you tell Her Highness?"

Kathy nodded, pulling herself upright. "Yes, of course. Thank you."

The stewardess disappeared, and Joachim, who had been curled up in the seat opposite his mother, stirred and sat up. He rubbed his eyes, which looked huge and tired and over-strained, and Kathy smiled at him. She thought he ought to be in bed, and wondered whether she should ask the stewardess for some hot milk. But just at that moment Natalia awoke too, and Kathy thought that perhaps, in a minute, she would ask her about the milk.

For a moment Natalia stared about her sleepily, then she opened her handbag, and taking a comb out began to drag it through her tousled hair. Staring at her own reflection in the mirror of her compact, she laughed and looked mischievously sideways at Kathy. "I wonder what my maid would say to me now?" she pondered.

Kathy smiled, and hoped the cheerful mood would last. She picked up her own bag and began to repair her make-up . . . then she suddenly remembered about the touch-down in Genoa. She told the Princess about it, and didn't notice the little silence that fell as she herself went on powdering her nose, and frowning over the application of her rose-pink lipstick.

Suddenly, Natalia said: "There isn't anything wrong, is there . . . really?"

"Of course not, madame . . . of course not." Kathy put her lipstick away in her bag, and snapped it shut. "The stewardess was quite definite. She didn't know why we were landing, but there is nothing wrong."

"No, no, I see. But why . . . ? I wonder . . ."

She was tense again, and almost inaudibly Kathy sighed.

And then a voice began to address them over the loudspeaker.

"Ladies and gentlemen, in five minutes' time we shall be landing in Genoa. Please fasten your seatbelts. No smoking will be allowed aboard the aircraft until after we have landed."

And monotonously, the message was repeated in other languages. *"Mesdames, messieurs . . ."* *"Signore, signori . . ."* They fastened their safety-belts, and through the windows they began to see the lights of Genoa. On one side Kathy caught a glimpse of shining water, and knew that it was the Mediterranean. She wondered how long they would have to wait, and whether they would be asked to leave the aircraft. That wouldn't be very good for the children.

The plane shuddered to a standstill, and in the sudden silence as the engines were cut only one or two quiet voices could be heard speaking.

And then a stewardess—the same stewardess who had spoken to Kathy earlier—came up to them. She smiled at the Princess deferentially.

"Madame, if you would like to leave the aircraft . . . there is a gentleman . . ."

"I will see no one."

Natalia's eyes were wide, her face suddenly ashen, and she was so plainly terrified that Kathy felt embarrassed.

"Her Highness does not—" she began, and then she recognized the man who was just entering the plane through a door at the other end of the long cabin. And at the same moment Natalia recognized him also, and Kathy heard her gasp.

"*Leonid!*" she whispered, and slowly the colour flooded back into her face, until it was deeply, rosily red.

Kathy fumbled with her safety-belt, but she couldn't undo it. Her fingers seemed numb, and deftly the stewardess helped her with it before stepping back as the Prince walked down the gangway towards them.

"Leonid, I . . ." Natalia seemed practically incapable of speech. Instinctively, Kathy stood up, and she felt the Prince's eyes dwelling on her coolly for a moment. Then he bowed, almost imperceptibly, to his sister-in-law.

"It is so fortunate, *petite*, that I was able to stop your plane. There is something that I feel you should know. I was sure you would not wish to continue on your way once you had heard my news. A small matter, but it could delay you for a day or two . . ."

He was speaking English, probably for the benefit of the stewardess, and one or two of the passengers looked round at him in curiosity. Everybody naturally wondered what was going on, and one or two people called for a stewardess to come and explain the situation. Leonid bent closer to his sister-in-law, and said something softly in a language which Kathy was beginning to recognize as Tirhanian. Natalia swallowed, but her colour was already beginning to return to normal, and she clutched at his hand and spoke rapidly in the same language. He answered in what seemed a decidedly soothing tone, then he straightened and looked at Kathy.

"Her Serene Highness and her children are leaving the aircraft," he said, and his voice was cold and detached. "They will be spending the night at a villa a few miles from Genoa. No doubt you will be accompanying them."

He was angry with her. In fact, he was furious. Kathy felt herself swallowing nervously, just as her employer had done. Quietly, she said: "Yes, Your Highness."

Two stewardesses helped to remove their light luggage from the rack, and meekly Natalia stood up while the Prince placed her coat about her shoulders. Nina was crying again, and Kathy picked her up, then held out her free hand to Joachim, who obligingly grasped at it this time without the smallest hesitation.

61

All the formalities of landing were, of course, got through with the maximum amount of speed, and outside the airport's main entrance a long white Jaguar was awaiting them. As Kathy relaxed on the rear seat with Nina on her lap, she realized for the first time that her head was aching, and she was grateful for the darkness inside the car, and for the fact that Leonid was sitting in the front beside the chauffeur, with his back to her. But she could just see the hard, angry outlines of his profile, fitfully illumined by the brilliant Italian street lighting, and it seemed to her that even the set of his shoulders expressed icy displeasure. She looked away from him, and out through the window at the tall white blocks of flats and the brightly lit cafés, and wondered how long she would be in Italy—how long, in fact, she would remain in Natalia's employment. Leonid was certainly her real employer, and Leonid had quite obviously made up his mind that however much she might please his sister-in-law, she was not a fit companion for a young woman who, as he had once said, required to be 'protected at all times', a childlike young woman who was, in his opinion, quite incapable of looking after herself. A young woman who, above all, was his own near relative—his responsibility.

So far, he had explained nothing—or at least he had explained nothing to Kathy—but quite obviously someone had told him about the Princess's flight from Paris, had managed to reach him, and stop him, before he had got too far on his way to take any personal action. And then he had interrupted his own journey so that he could have Natalia's plane brought down in Genoa.

Idly, Kathy wondered where they were going now, but she was really too tired, and too bewildered, to feel any very great interest. It was almost impossible to believe that only a little over twenty-four hours earlier she had simply been a receptionist at Ransome's Hotel in London. Since then so many things had happened to her that her memory was beginning to play tricks on her, and the jumble of impressions which filled her mind was so confused that she found it almost impossible to sort it out. Had she really flown from London to Paris and from Paris to Genoa? Had she really acquired a fantastic new Parisian wardrobe . . . a wardrobe which was at this moment lying in one of the most luxurious hotels in the French capital, waiting to be sent on to her? She remembered the midnight-blue evening dress, and wondered whether she would ever see it again. Not that it worried her very much, for the clothes she already possessed were really quite adequate for the sort of life she normally led, and would probably be leading again in a few days' time, and as she didn't feel she had any right whatsoever to the enormous salary cheque she had received she didn't feel she had any right to keep the clothes either.

It had all been a strange, vivid dream—a rather confused dream—but soon it would be over, and she would be back in London, looking for another job. She didn't suppose she would ever regret what had happened, for after all it had been a marvellous experience, or she supposed it had. But she did hope that it would all be over quickly, and that she would be able to leave for home in the morning.

For about ten minutes the car moved along broad, brightly-lit streets, and across handsome squares, and she supposed that they were travelling through the city of Genoa. Although it was now nearly midnight the streets were still very busy and packed with buses and gleaming Italian cars, but after a time the traffic thinned a little, the noise and confusion grew less, and glancing to her right Kathy saw that they were travelling along by the very edge of the Mediterranean. It was much warmer here in Italy than it had been in Paris, and the sky was clear and star-studded. A slender young moon hung over the harbour, and a ship that looked like a cruising liner lay at anchor a little way out, swimming in the reflection of its own myriad lights. Even above the roar of the car's engine it was possible to hear the heavy sighing of the waves on the unseen beach, and Kathy felt suddenly, strangely soothed. It was so peaceful, leaning back against the deliciously comfortable upholstery of the car, watching the faintly gleaming sea go by. Perhaps everything would be all right after all . . .

She was almost asleep when the car suddenly turned off the road, and as she awoke with a start she realized that they were passing between tall iron gates. Beyond the gates lay a drive, a winding, narrow drive that was bordered by a dense profusion of unfamiliar trees and shrubs, and which climbed steadily for about a quarter of a mile before finally coming to an end in front of a house, a house which was long, and low, and rather Moorish-looking, and which was a blaze of golden light. A flight of steps led from the gravel sweep in front of the house to a doorway which was set rather high up in the wall, and at the foot of these steps the car came to rest.

Leonid got out. Framed in the doorway at the top of the steps was an elderly woman, and with hands outstretched he walked quickly up to meet her. She was certainly well over seventy, and she leant rather heavily on a thin ebony cane, but nevertheless as the Prince reached her she sank down in a skilfully executed, old-fashioned curtsy, and it was only when he had helped her up and hugged her with surprising enthusiasm that she became less formal, and kissed him on both cheeks.

By this time the chauffeur had opened the rear doors of the car, and Leonid came down to help his sister-in-law alight. She had hardly spoken a word during the journey from the airport, and she looked white and tired. He took her arm and helped her up the steps, and at the top the older woman received them. They all vanished into the house, and Kathy supposed that she and the children had better follow their example. They seemed to have forgotten about the children, both of whom were fast asleep in the back of the car. She lifted Nina out, and the chauffeur, who was middle-aged and kindly, took Joachim. Together they climbed the steps, and at the top Kathy stood still. But immediately a feminine voice uttered an exclamation, then addressed her in the strange tongue which was probably Tirhanian. It was the old lady whom the Prince had hugged, and as Kathy looked at her uncomprehendingly she made a little clucking sound, and tugged at an old-fashioned bell-rope which hung beside the door.

"But of course, you are English! An English governess, yes? I am sorry, my dear, at first I did not realize . . . But one has only to look at you! Come in, come in, and bring the poor little ones. To think I had forgotten them!"

Kathy stepped over the threshold into the warmth and brightness of a large square hall. The floor was of white marble, strewn with colourful rugs, and there was a lot of heavy, ornate furniture about, giving the place rather the look of a museum. Or so it seemed to Kathy, as she stood just inside the doorway, almost swaying on her feet . . . and still holding the slumbrous Nina.

From somewhere at the back of the hall a small, neat maid appeared, and the old lady gestured towards Kathy and the children and said something rapidly in Italian. In English, she added: "Rosa will show you where the children are to sleep. And then, when you have put them to bed, she will show you your own room."

As Kathy looked faintly bewildered the old lady added: "The Princess has already been taken to her apartments. If you should wish to speak with her, Rosa will show you where she is."

It seemed utterly pointless to protest that she was not the children's governess—in any case, as Natalia and Leonid had abandoned them to her care, that seemed to be precisely what she was . . . for the time being, at any rate. And somebody had to look after them.

So she thanked the old lady, who said something in Italian to the chauffeur who was still carrying Joachim, and together they followed the maid along endless corridors—there was no staircase, and almost every room in the villa seemed to be on the one floor —until they reached a long, white-walled room which had obviously been fitted up as a children's night-nursery. It contained three narrow white beds, two of which had been made up and turned down for the night, and the tall windows were guarded by white wooden shutters. A deep, soft ice-blue carpet covered every inch of floor space, and there were little white basket-work chairs, and a bookcase full of gaily-bound children's books.

The chauffeur gently deposited the sleepy Joachim on one of the beds, and turned to beam at Kathy.

"Buona notte, signorina." Then he sketched a salute, and was gone.

The maid went round the room testing radiators, in an attempt to make sure that the right amount of heat was being generated, but she need hardly have bothered, for the room was almost oppressively warm, and in fact Kathy felt that she would have liked to throw a window open.

"The Princess . . ." she said. "She is . . . ?"

"At the end of the corridor, *signorina.* Ring, please, when you are ready, and I will come and show you. I will show you your own room also, but you will wish to attend to the small ones first, no?" Her English was surprisingly good.

A little wearily, Kathy agreed that she would 'attend to the small ones first,' and that when she was ready she would ring. The maid left the room, and Kathy sank down on one of the children's beds and gave herself a little shake. She was completely exhausted, and her head ached more than ever now, but she knew that she had to pull herself together, for there was no one else to look after the children, or at least, no one who seemed prepared to look after them. With as much firmness as she could muster, she stifled a slight feeling of resentment which had

67

begun to assail her. All this was a wonderful, fantastic experience, and whatever happened she should be grateful to Leonid and the Princess for having given it to her.

And in the morning no doubt she would be grateful. Resolutely, she stood up. In one hand the chauffeur had carried up the children's suitcase, and she knelt down and opened it, looking for their pyjamas. The maid had suggested bringing them warm milk and biscuits, but they were both too sleepy, and in fact they were still fast asleep, one on each bed. With any luck she should be able to get them both into bed without waking them up.

Twenty minutes later they were both comfortably tucked up, and neither had stirred, so she rang the bell for the maid. And when a further ten minutes had elapsed, and no maid had appeared, she wandered out into the corridor, quietly closing the door behind her. It was warm and very still in the corridor as she wandered along it, and there didn't seem to be a single sound emerging from behind any of the doors she passed, so she was all the more surprised when, just as she reached the point where the corridor merged with the huge, square hall, a voice suddenly spoke her name. It was a masculine voice, and it was tinged with an accent that was definitely foreign. It was the voice of Prince Leonid.

She jumped perceptibly, and turned, to see him standing in front of a doorway on the other side of the hall. He looked rather drawn, she thought, but not exactly tired, and he was eyeing her with something akin to distaste.

"Miss Grant! If you don't mind, I should like to speak with you."

He stood aside from the doorway, and indicated that he wished her to pass him, and when she did so she found herself in a long room which was lined with books. The floor was covered with more of the brightly coloured rugs which she had noticed in the hall, and there was a good deal of dark, highly polished furniture about, and several rather handsome crimson leather armchairs.

Leonid followed her into the room, and when he had closed the door behind him, he walked over to the empty marble fireplace, and stood staring thoughtfully down at the antique fire-screen which concealed the bareness of the grate. He didn't suggest that Kathy should sit down, and in fact he allowed nearly a minute to elapse before he said anything at all. Then he lifted his dark head and looked at her, and his eyes were quite expressionless.

"You may remember, *mademoiselle*, that before leaving London we had a small talk, you and I."

"Yes . . . yes, I remember."

"I explained to you that my sister-in-law was in need of protection . . . I should have said, partly from herself, but I assumed that you understood me. I arrived in Paris, and was greeted by an urgent message from my own country—it was important that I should be able to get home as quickly as possible. So I left Natalia in your care—because you seemed to me to be a sensible and efficient young woman—and I arranged for an old and trusted friend of mine, who happens to be attached to the Embassy in Paris, to escort you both as far as Rome. Once you had arrived there, I intended to decide myself whether you should proceed any farther at present."

His hands behind his back, he began to pace up and down the long room. "But Natalia does not like this arrangement . . . She thinks that she would prefer to dispense with the society of my friend, Colonel Zanin. And you, *mademoiselle*, you do not lift a finger to check her—you do not attempt to discourage her. You yourself, or so I am informed, booked the seats on the aircraft." He laughed shortly and harshly. "A pair of irresponsible school girls . . . indulging in an undignified escapade while in charge of two small children!"

He stopped his pacing up and down, and stood still, only two or three feet away from her. His eyes in his rather narrow face were hard and questioning, and he looked as if he were awaiting an explanation.

Kathy stared back at him, blinking a little, and her own eyes felt prickly with fatigue. She wanted to tell him that she had tried . . . that she had done her best to be calm and sensible, and prevent Natalia leaving Paris without her appointed escort, but somehow the words wouldn't come. She wondered why the lines of books on the shelves in front of her seemed to be expanding and contracting, and why even the accusing black eyes staring so hard into her own didn't seem to be so very distinct any more. As if from a long distance away, she heard her own voice saying:

"I'm sorry . . . I really am sorry, Your Highness . . ."

And then the world went dark, and she was spinning round, and falling . . . falling . . .

When she awoke, she was lying on a crimson leather sofa, and someone was bending over her, pressing a glass to her lips. Whoever it was who held the glass they had evidently been trying to force its contents down her throat, and because she couldn't be bothered to put up much in the way of opposition she swallowed some of the liquid—and immediately regretted it, for it burnt her throat and made her cough. Her eyes flew open, and she made an attempt to sit up, but instantly a firm hand was placed on her shoulder, and a quiet voice said:

"No, you must not get up yet. Soon you will feel much better, but you must be still."

She looked up into the face of the man who was standing beside her, and saw that it was Leonid. Instantly, she made another effort to struggle up, and again he restrained her.

"No, you must rest." He shook his head at her, and his voice was quietly authoritative—the voice of a man who simply did not expect to be disobeyed. He sat down on the side of the sofa and lit a cigarette . . . and inconsequentially Kathy thought that he must smoke a great deal more than was good for him.

"Poor child!" he said suddenly, staring down at her. "Were you so very tired, or is it that you are afraid of me?"

"I . . . I was rather tired," she confessed. Then: "Did I really faint?" she asked shyly. "I'm terribly sorry!"

One of his hands moved slightly in a dismissing gesture.

"It was not your fault." He drew on his cigarette, and surveyed her thoughtfully over the top of it. "I should have seen that you had 'had enough,' as you would say."

For the first time since coming to herself, Kathy remembered exactly what had happened, and what

Leonid had been saying to her during the last few moments before everything seemed to turn dark. A faint hint of colour entered her cheeks, and in a small voice she said painfully:

"I really am sorry about . . . about what happened. I know that I should have been able to talk the Princess out of leaving Paris without your friend, but—"

"We will not discuss it any more. When I think about it, I see it is obvious that you could have done nothing. There is something which I have not yet asked you . . . What is your age, Miss Grant?"

"Twenty." This time the flush was noticeable, and she wondered when he was going to tell her that his sister-in-law would no longer require her services.

"Twenty!" he repeated quietly. "It is not very old. And Natalia is twenty-three . . . a widow with two children. Could you handle her, do you think, *mademoiselle*?"

"I . . ." She hesitated. "I—I could have tried. But she is . . . who she is, and—"

"And you are young, and English, and a little timid, and you are not accustomed to being in a position of authority, I think." He gave her another long look, and then stood up and stubbed out his cigarette. "To me, Natalia is a child . . . sweet-tempered, easily guided. I had not realized that she could appear differently to someone like you."

Before he could prevent her, Kathy slipped her feet to the ground and stood up. "Your Highness," she said with sudden firmness, "I understand perfectly that you have to dismiss me. I'm sorry that— that I turned out to be so unsatisfactory. I did my best, but I'm simply not the right sort of person for the job. And now I really would like to go to bed, if you don't mind."

"Naturally I don't mind. But I don't wish to dismiss you."

She looked up at him in astonishment. "You don't? But . . ."

"I have other concerns," he said rather wearily. For the first time she noticed the strain in his eyes, the lines of fatigue about his firm mouth. "My sister-in-law likes you," he went on, "and she trusts you. At least she is happier now that you are with her. I was entirely wrong to blame you for what happened this afternoon . . . you could not have prevented it. Early tomorrow morning—no, later today," glancing at his watch, "I shall be leaving for Tirhania, but the Princess and her children will be staying here, and I shall feel happier if you stay with them."

Amazed, she murmured: "Thank you, Your Highness."

"Your hostess here is Signora Albinhieri . . . who is my godmother, and has a fondness for all my family. You will find her very kind."

"I think I have already met her."

"Good." He came closer and stood looking down at her, studying the violet eyes, dark with exhaustion, and the little smudgy shadows beneath them. "You are all right now, Miss Grant? You will not faint again?"

She did feel a little dazed, but she shook her head valiantly. "No, of course not, Your Highness. I don't know why I fainted this evening—I've never done such a thing in my life before."

"But you were so very tired." He smiled at her, and it was the charming smile she remembered. "And

73

now you must certainly go to bed, but before I ring for the maid I have two more things to say to you."

"Yes?" Her eyes were frankly sleepy.

"First I do not like to call you Miss Grant. What is your first name . . . I mean, your Christian name?"

"Kathy," she said automatically.

"Then you are . . . Katherine, are you not?"

"Yes."

"With your permission, I will call you Katherine."

"Of course, if you wish to, Your Highness."

"And the second thing I have to say to you is that to you I am not 'Your Highness.' So many times this evening you have said it, but I am not a person in an operetta, and if you please you will merely address me as *'monsieur.'* "

"Yes . . . yes, *monsieur.*"

"Thank you, and now I will ring for the maid, and carry you to your room, for you will not, I think, be able to walk so far."

She gasped, and uttered a small protest, but he ignored it, and when the maid Rosa appeared in almost immediate response to the summons of the bell he picked Kathy up, and disregarding her rather feeble assurances that she was perfectly capable of walking, bore her lightly along the corridors to her own room. Once there, he set her down, and spoke to the maid in Italian. Then he turned back to Kathy, and accorded her a slight bow.

"Goodbye, Katherine. In a few days we shall meet again. In the meantime, I trust you!"

"Thank you, *monsieur.*"

The maid, obviously acting on instructions, wanted to remain and assist her into bed, but Kathy refused to let her, and in fact was relieved when the door closed on Rosa, and at last she was alone. The small suitcase which she had brought with her from Paris had been brought up and placed at the foot of the bed, and it didn't take her long to find a night-dress, slip out of her clothes, and climb wearily between Signora Albinhieri's cool, faintly scented sheets.

Vaguely, she wondered what had been happening to the Princess, but she knew Natalia would be in good hands . . . she didn't need to worry. She didn't feel like worrying about anything, for despite her weariness she was conscious of being strangely happy.

She sighed, and turned out the light, and within two minutes was fast asleep.

CHAPTER SIX

A few hours later Kathy awoke to find a small, frightened-looking maid—not Rosa—standing beside her bed. The girl spoke a little English, and was very apologetic.

"I knock on the door," she explained agitatedly, "but the *signorina* does not wake! And the *signora*, she says that the *signorina* must come quickly, please!"

Kathy struggled up, pushing her tumbled hair out of her eyes. Automatically, she glanced at her wrist-watch. It was four a.m.

"The *signora* . . . ?" She forced herself to wake up properly. "What has happened?"

The girl looked more frightened than ever. "There is something bad on the telephone, *signorina*. It is for the *principessa* . . . the Signora Albinhieri has told her. She wishes that you will go to her now."

Kathy jumped out of bed, her pulses hammering, a constricted feeling in her throat. She was only too wide awake now . . . She felt cold with fear, despite the presence in the room of three red-hot radiators, and was grateful for the comforting warmth of her old quilted dressing-gown, as she slipped it on and wrapped it about her. Outside in the corridors all the lights were burning, and as she and the maid hurried towards the Princess's room, it was possible to hear sounds of activity far off on the other side of the villa. Somewhere a telephone rang shrilly, and almost immediately it was answered. What could be happening? Kathy, pale and slightly trembling, remembering

Leonid on the way to Rome, didn't want to think.

When they reached the Princess's room the maid knocked lightly on the door, and from inside a feminine voice instructed them to enter. Kathy stepped inside, and the maid, having done her duty, fled.

Natalia's room was spacious and beautiful, and might have been designed expressly for her—as possibly it had been. The spreading cream-coloured carpet flowed like a pale sea into every tiny corner, and the curtains that hid the tall shuttered windows were golden, and made of shimmering silk. Everything in the room gave an impression of lightness and incomparable elegance, even to the antique French bed with its quilted headboard, and there were gilt-framed mirrors and Sévres ornaments, and on a low table a silver bowl filled with white hot-house roses.

All of this Kathy automatically noticed, as she stood, for a second or so, just inside the door. And then the stately elderly woman who had greeted her a few hours earlier rose from a chair and came towards her, and looking past her Kathy saw Natalia, seated on a low sofa.

Signora Albinhieri leaned a little towards Kathy, and her voice, as she spoke, was very soft. "She sent for you, my child . . . You are a good friend to her, I think. You have heard the news?"

Wordlessly, Kathy shook her head, and the old lady sighed.

"Simply that which we have all feared. A rebel government has control of Tirhania."

Bewildered, Kathy stared at the old lady, but she only gestured towards Natalia. "Remain with her . . . I have much to do."

And then she was gone, the door closing softly behind her, and Kathy stood still, savouring the knowledge that the news was nothing to do with Leonid, and feeling extraordinarily light-headed with relief. Then she looked at her employer. "Madame . . ." she began gently.

Natalia looked up. She was white and haggard-looking, and her hands shook. "You know . . . ?" she asked. Her voice, from between colourless lips, was a pathetic thread of sound.

"Yes, I know." Kathy sat down beside her, and covered one of the other woman's hands with her own. "Are you all right, madame? Would you like something . . . a cup of coffee . . . some brandy?"

"No, thank you." She smoothed her hair and moistened her lips. "It is so warm in here—could you open the window, please?"

Kathy pulled aside the heavy golden curtains, and then found herself obliged to struggle with what seemed to be several layers of white-painted shutters. But at last she succeeded in wrenching a window open, and the sweet, cool air of the last hour before dawn began to seep into the room.

Natalia joined her at the window. "I heard that you put the children to bed," she said. "I am sorry. I did not wish that it should be necessary for you to do that."

"That's all right," said Kathy. A faint, whispering breeze stirred her hair, and she wondered whether this fresh morning air could really be good for Natalia at the moment. "It's a little cold, madame," she ventured, "and you've had rather a shock. Don't you think that perhaps—"

"No, I will stay here. It is very good of you, *chérie*, to be concerned for me, but I cannot bear the warmth of this room, and indeed I am quite all right now."

She smiled at Kathy, and although the smile was a little taut, and strain showed in every line of her small white face, she really did seem calm. Kathy longed to ask questions, but she felt she had no right to, and so she fell uncomfortably silent. She felt chilled and numb and very slightly sick, as for the first time she began to appreciate the full meaning and implications of what the *signora* had said. Something terrible has happened in Tirhania . . . A *coup d'état*, the sort of thing one normally only heard of in radio or television news bulletins, or saw blazoned across the front pages of the papers. It was not the sort of thing in which one ever imagined oneself becoming involved . . . at least, not if one were a young Englishwoman, and had been born and brought up, as she had, in a country vicarage.

A week ago, it would have meant practically nothing to her. Today, it was vitally important, because it would almost certainly alter the whole lives of people like Natalia and Leonid . . . Leonid! Suddenly the cold, sick feeling increased. Would Leonid be safe? She swallowed. After all, she had been talking to him only last night—or had it been this morning?—and she didn't—naturally she didn't want to think that anything could have happened . . . not to Leonid. He had been angry with her at one time, but he had also been kind. Surely . . . surely he wouldn't fly on to Tirhania despite reports of the *coup*?

The Princess broke into her thoughts. "Leonid will be coming back here. He did get as far as Rome,

79

but apparently he was not able to travel farther. All the airfields in Tirhania have been closed."

Kathy drew a long, sighing breath of relief. "I'm glad," she said. "Then the Prince will be safe?"

"Yes, he will be safe." The Princess's face was smooth and curiously untroubled, and very beautiful, like a face carved in ivory. "Anton, he is safe also. With his wife, he escaped yesterday, I understand."

"Then all your family is safe madame?"

"Yes, I am fortunate."

There was a light rap on the door, and Signora Albinhieri came into the room. She looked anxious, but at sight of Natalia's unusually controlled features an expression of unmistakable relief passed across her own.

"Child," she said, looking at Natalia, "go back to bed, and rest. There is nothing more to be said or done until Leonid returns from Rome."

Rather to Kathy's surprise, Natalia meekly allowed herself to be assisted back into bed, and agreed that if a cup of coffee were to be sent for she would drink it. She looked very small and frail when she was propped up against the enormous lace-edged pillows which seemed common to most of the bedrooms in the villa, but there was no doubt about it: she *was* calm. At least, she did not appear to be in the grip of any particularly violent distress.

Signora Albinhieri nodded at Kathy. "Come, Miss Grant."

The Princess did not raise any objections to Kathy's leaving the room, so she obeyed, but outside the door, in the softly carpeted corridor, she hesitated, and the *signora* looked at her piercingly.

"You are young," she remarked, "and I do not think you are used to being involved in such situations as this. But then I am old, and for many years I have led a life so peaceful that I had forgotten what it is like to be close to a royal household. We shall both have to be courageous, Miss Grant. The next few days will be a strain upon all of us in this house."

"Yes, I realize that, *signora*," said Kathy quietly.

"Well, go to your room, and get what rest you can. If you are needed I will send for you. Otherwise I would suggest that at eight o'clock you join me for breakfast in the *sala da pranzo*."

"Yes, *signora*."

The old lady began to walk away, but at the last moment she hesitated, and turned back.

"By the way, *signorina*, I am told that you are not a governess. Forgive me. This morning you will not trouble with the *bambini*. The maids will attend to them."

"Oh, but I don't mind, really . . ."

"Nevertheless, your other duties will be quite sufficiently burdensome. The Princess will need you, *signorina* . . . all the time. There will be letters to be answered—practical work to be done. You will have little time for the children, believe me."

Back in her own room, Kathy went across to one of the windows, and flung the heavy shutters wide, as she had done in Natalia's room. Then she pushed the window open.

The darkness was just beginning to lift, and she realized that she could see the Mediterranean, pearl grey and luminous in the first glimmer of morning light. She could see that the villa was very high—as she had known it must be—and the slopes beneath it seemed clothed with a dark and impenetrable jungle of trees. Here and there a tall, narrow cypress stood out like a shadowy pencil against the pale shimmer of the quiet sea, and a little way away, to the right, she glimpsed the top of a tower—perhaps a bell-tower. And even as she listened, she caught the faint, clear beckoning notes of the bell itself. Six o'clock . . . The Angelus. Far away in the distance there was a sound of roaring, hurrying traffic, and she guessed that it must come from the great coast road along which she had travelled the night before— the road which, she supposed, probably followed the entire length of the Italian Riviera.

It was strange and exciting and wonderful, to be here in Italy, but this morning Kathy's heart felt heavy with sympathy for the Karanska family, and her mind was in a turmoil which even the hazy, silver-grey beauty of the Italian winter dawn could not smooth. Determinedly, she closed the windows, and went back to lie down on her bed. She was still very tired after the previous day, and she owed it to her employer to be as fresh as possible during the trying time that presumably lay ahead of them all.

At eight o'clock, Kathy breakfasted with the *signora*, in the *sala da pranzo*. There was nobody else present, and the room was big and impressive, and rather cold—possibly because in the general excitement the central heating system had not been receiving sufficient attention.

The breakfast consisted of coffee and rolls . . . a type of breakfast which Kathy could not remember ever having sampled in her life before, but which she found to be completely delectable. The coffee was very hot, and served with jugs of steaming milk, and the rolls, which were eaten with butter and a selection of excellent preserves, were fresh and delicious. She found herself enjoying the meal a good deal more than she could remember having enjoyed the dinner which had been served to her on the plane the night before, and by the time she had consumed three rolls, and refused a fourth cup of coffee, she felt considerably better.

Pale December sunshine slanted through the windows on to the grey marble of the floor, and at sight of it her spirits automatically lifted. She felt suddenly capable of coping with anything that might lie ahead of her.

At last the old lady consumed the last of her coffee, and stood up briskly. "It is quiet," she observed. "I have instructed the telephone exchange that they are to put no more calls through to us at the moment. And it has been arranged that all the gates of the villa should be guarded by *carabinieri*, so that if representatives of the Press should arrive in person, as they certainly will, they will be unable to gain entry."

Kathy's eyes grew rather large. "I hadn't thought . . ." she began. "I suppose this . . . will be in all the papers, won't it?"

"My dear child," said the *signora*, walking over to one of the windows, "the entire world is talking of Tirhania this morning. Some, of course, are shocked by the news, other are pleased. It is a question of beliefs. Either one is a monarchist or one is not. Most people, however, feel some sort of interest in the plight of a young and beautiful widow who has been driven from her homeland, and I make no doubt that for the next few days—perhaps even for the next few weeks—we in this house will be under siege. And remember, Miss Grant"—the old eyes bright and penetrating as she swung round to look searchingly at Kathy—"whatever you may be told, by the Princess or anyone else in this house, whatever you may perhaps overhear, it is confidential, and must be repeated to nobody. You understand me?"

"Of course. I wouldn't—I couldn't—repeat anything, *signora*."

"Good." The eyes still hovered on Kathy's face. "Good, my child." And then there was the sound of a car drawing up somewhere close to the windows, and Signora Albinhieri looked out.

"It is Leonid," she said, and the note of relief in her voice was quite unmistakable. "Go and rouse Natalia, my dear. The Prince will wish to see his sister-in-law . . . and no doubt she will wish to see him."

Kathy obeyed, and she was just crossing the entrance hall when Leonid came through the front door, his beautifully cut grey suit a little creased, his face pale and his eyes appallingly haggard. As he caught sight of Kathy the furrow which the last few hours had etched deepened a little between his brows, but all he said was: "Good morning, Miss Grant."

Kathy longed to say something—just something—to show him that she realized what a terrible thing it was that had happened, to make him understand what tremendous sympathy she felt for him just then. But the expression on his face frightened her in its grim remoteness, and she suddenly felt very small and insignificant and foolish . . . an unimportant little English girl to whom Leonid of Tirhania was and would always be as remote as the planet Mars. How could she understand what a man of his type must be going through at such a time as this . . . how could she begin to enter in to his feelings. It was impossible—even to express sympathy would be an intrusion, an impertinence. So she whispered a hasty 'good morning' and hurried past him on her way to the Princess's room.

The rest of the morning passed uneventfully. Natalia had a short interview with the Prince, and then went on resting in her room, and Leonid vanished into the long library, in which Kathy had fainted the night before, and sent for the male secretary who formed part of his suite. There was nothing of any importance for Kathy to do, so she wandered along to the nursery, to where she found both the children being entertained by the large, beaming housemaid in whose care they had temporarily been placed. Later in the day, some of the staff who had been left in Paris would be arriving, but for the moment the maid Luisa was to be responsible for their creature comforts. Kathy decided that she might as well take them for a short walk, and as soon as the maid understood that the *signorina* meant to relieve her of her responsibilities for a while she sprang up from the floor, where she had been crawling in evident imitation of a bear, and departed with alacrity in the direction of the kitchens, where a large cup of coffee and a comfortable gossip would no doubt be awaiting her.

Kathy took the children out on to the terrace. She supposed it would not be wise for them to wander too far into the grounds, in case they should be set upon by a marauding reporter—though it still seemed rather ridiculous to suppose that any reporter might be lying in wait for the opportunity of questioning her—so they stayed close to the white walls of the house, and Joachim found a rather grubby tennis ball, which someone had probably dropped by accident, and amused himself by bouncing it up and down on the white, scrubbed flags of the terrace. Nina ran around in circles, admiring the flowers, and the wonderful tree covered in oranges that stood just below the terrace. And then she tired, and had to be picked up. Joachim soon grew tired too, and Kathy thought he looked pale and dispirited—almost as if he realized that something was wrong. She wondered what sort of things he thought about, and how soon somebody would decide to tell him that he might not, after all, grow up to be a king.

She took them back indoors, saw that they washed their hands in readiness for lunch, then sat on the floor and leafed through Italian picture-books with them until Luisa returned to serve and supervize their lunch. Then she left them, and went back to her own room.

Considerably to her relief she found that lunch was not being served in the *sala da pranzo* that day, but in the guests' own apartments, and when she had eaten as much as she could manage of the pleasant, light meal which was brought to her on a tray by Rosa, she lay down on her bed and attempted to enjoy a siesta.

Far off in the house she could hear continuous quiet, unobtrusive sounds, but they were mainly muted by distance and lavish carpeting, and she was almost asleep by the time a hand rapped sharply on her door, and in response to her murmured 'come in' Rosa looked in at her.

"*Scusa, signorina*, but there is gentleman to see you. He is in the *salon*."

"A *gentleman*?" repeated Kathy in bewilderment, wondering at the same time whether it would ever be possible to sleep for any length of time in this bewildering place.

"Yes, *signorina*. He says he is from the British Con-sul-ate, and if you do not mind he would like to see you."

The British Consulate! Kathy got up. "Tell the gentleman I will come in a moment, Rosa."

She ran a comb through her hair, lightly dusted her nose with powder, and applied a sparing touch of lipstick to her mouth. Then she walked along the corridor and into the huge, handsome room which she had already discovered was known as the *salon*.

A young man was standing by the fireplace—a tall, very English-looking young man, whose eyes registered distinct surprise when Kathy walked into the room. Then their expression altered, as she walked towards him, to reveal something more like undisguised admiration.

"Miss Grant?"

"That's right."

"Well, I'm Robert Markham. I'm from the Consulate in Mirano, and I've been sent to find out whether or not you're all right."

She smiled, feeling suddenly relaxed. It was so nice to hear an English voice.

"Thank you, but I'm perfectly all right, Mr. Markham."

"You're quite sure? You see, we heard about you, and it didn't seem right for an English girl to be shut up here with all this going on." He waved a hand in a gesture which he had probably picked up since coming to Italy. "The Press are a mile deep outside the main gate, you know. To get in at all I had to put my foot down and charge!"

"It's not as bad as that in here . . . we're very quiet." She asked him to sit down, and he did so, at the same time offering her a cigarette, which she refused. She found the concentrated approval in his grey eyes rather embarrassing, but at the same time it was very pleasant to be sitting opposite anyone with whom she could talk more or less on equal terms.

"How do you like Italy?" He asked the question casually, glancing around him at the splendours of the room in which they sat.

"Very much—I think. I only arrived here last night, and there's been so much to think about . . ."

He looked at her sharply. "Don't worry about the Karanskas. They've nothing to fear. The revolution was absolutely bloodless, and provided they don't feel tempted to go back and try to alter things they'll be perfectly safe. You're employed by Princess Natalia, aren't you?"

"Yes."

"Well, I don't suppose there's any possibility that she will want to go back."

They talked for a few minutes more and then, with transparent reluctance, Robert Markham stood up to go.

"We'll be keeping an eye on you," he told her. "And if anything worries you, don't hesitate to get in touch with me at the Consulate."

She nodded. "I won't forget."

When he had gone, she walked over to the window, and watched him drive away in a small white sports car. It was nice to know that there was someone in the district to whom she could turn.

The next few days went by rather peacefully—remarkably peacefully, Kathy thought. Shoals of newspapers, both Italian and foreign, found their way into the villa, and from what she could understand of their contents Kathy gathered that the troubles in Tirhania were headline news all over the world, but inside the Villa Albinhieri everything remained quiet. Natalia, for the first day or two stunned and bewildered, gradually began to return to normal, and when the new dresses she had ordered in Paris duly arrived as if nothing had happened, she seemed to derive the keenest pleasure from trying them on and pirouetting before the long gilt-framed mirrors in her bedroom. Kathy's new clothes arrived as well, and she too was conscious of a definite satisfaction as she tried on the champagne-coloured silk and the dark, diaphanous evening dress, and filled her drawers with soft, pastel-hued twin-sets and mountains of lacy underwear.

The children, particularly Joachim, were good and rather quiet, and every day they played for a while on the terrace, under the supervision of Kathy or Luisa . . . and every afternoon spent an hour with their mother, in the beautiful white and gold *sala* which was reserved for her personal use.

Kathy saw little of Leonid, and for his part he seemed rather to avoid her than otherwise. She invariably had her meals with Natalia, in the latter's sitting-room, and at most other times of the day the Prince seemed perennially occupied in the library, telephoning and dictating letters.

On the fourth evening, however, Natalia suddenly decided that she would dine with the others, and if she did so, then Kathy would have to do so too, for she must have moral support.

Kathy would very much have liked to back out, for she felt that at this private family dinner her presence could only be an intrusion—especially at a time when there must be so much that the Karanskas would like to discuss among themselves—but she was not allowed to think of it, so she attired herself in a rather prim lavender-coloured cocktail dress which she had possessed since before she left England, and at seven-forty-five duly went along to the *salon*, where she had been told it was the custom for guests at the Villa to assemble before dinner.

When she entered the room, she found the Prince and Signora Albinhieri already there, but Natalia, evidently, had not yet appeared. As soon as Kathy came in, Leonid, immaculate in a dinner-jacket of irreproachable cut, announced that he would prepare her a drink, and suddenly overcome with shyness and self-consciousness, she agreed to accept a small sherry.

He did not say anything as he handed her the small, fragile Venetian goblet in which the sherry danced and sparkled like tawny, liquid fire, but as she took it from him and murmured a 'thank you' she instinctively glanced up into his face, and saw that his eyes were cold and quellingly remote. Feeling chilled and dispirited, she sipped at the sherry, then put it down on the table which Leonid had just courteously moved to a position close to her elbow. The silence, she thought, might have lasted for ever had it been left to herself and the Prince, but fortunately Signora Albinhieri was there to break it. Her bright eyes had been surveying Kathy with interest and a certain amount of curiosity ever since the English girl had entered the *salon*, and she appeared to be voicing an opinion she could keep to herself no longer when she suddenly said:

"My dear, you are very charming tonight. Is she not, Leon?"

Kathy felt herself colouring vividly, and was furious with herself. She didn't look up, for she didn't want to see those cold, masculine eyes surveying her with critical appraisal. Feeling like an unusually foolish schoolgirl, she said quietly:

"Thank you, *signora*."

The Prince said nothing. Smiling rather archly, Signora Albinhieri sipped her drink in silence. Then she said:

"Soon, I am afraid, you will be becoming bored. No doubt you are accustomed to being surrounded by admiring young men . . . here, there is no one even to take you to the theatre in Genoa. It is a situation which is quite deplorable!" Again, the old lady sipped at her drink, while Kathy felt the flush spreading to her neck and ears.

"I assure, you, *signora*, I'm not accustomed to being surrounded by admiring young men, and I don't want to be taken out . . ." Her voice sounded stiff with embarrassment.

"So!" The old eyes twinkled. "There is one man in particular, yes? But of course, that is it! You have a—what do you call it—an understanding. You are

91

affianced, perhaps. These things are handled so strangely in England these days. But customs vary, and I daresay you find it quite romantic. Does he write to you . . . ? If he should wish to come here, of course you may receive him at any time you wish!"

"Really, *signora*, there is no one!" Kathy lifted a hand to her scarlet cheek, miserably conscious of the Prince's gaze, bent intently upon her.

But to her surprise, Leonid was the next to speak. "I do not think, *marraine*, that we have any right to enquire into the personal life of Miss Grant."

There was detachment and disinterest in his tone, combined with a note of distaste which seemed to indicate that her display of schoolgirlish self-consciousness had been rather more than he could stand. It was bad enough, he seemed to be thinking, to be obliged to dine with his sister-in-law's little English companion; to be forced to discuss her private affairs and pursue the question of whether or not she had a fiancé awaiting her in England would be quite insupportable.

The subject was dropped then, in any case, for Natalia came in in a floating creation of golden net, and very soon afterwards they all adjourned to the dining-room.

Dinner was long-drawn-out and elaborately served, and the conversation moved lightly and smoothly around a number of trifling subjects which were of no very great importance to anybody present, and so were completely safe and proper topics for general discussion. Leonid took little part, she noticed, but she herself was skilfully drawn in by Natalia and Signora Albinhieri, and the ease and fluency with which they undertook the courtesy of invariably speaking nothing but English in her presence never ceased to amaze her. Signora Albinhieri said nothing further to embarrass her, and by the time they left the dining-table, shortly after nine o'clock, she felt more or less at ease. She did not even feel particularly alarmed when, after handing her her coffee cup in the adjoining *salon*, Leonid sat down beside her.

After all, she thought, his disapprobation meant very little to her. It really didn't matter in the least what he thought of her . . . she wasn't afraid of him. But when she stole a sideways glance at him she saw that his face was not nearly as forbidding as it had seemed earlier in the evening, and although there was something curiously alert in the dark eyes as they rested on her, there was also a hint of unaccustomed softness.

"You are pale," he said, but something in his voice robbed the remark of any suggestion of criticism. "Are you well . . . happy here? You do not find it too trying that you are not permitted to go beyond the gardens?"

"No, of course not, I . . . love it here. I think I'm really very lucky—there are such wonderful gardens to walk in. And it's marvellous just to know that I'm in Italy." She dropped her eyes, suddenly disconcerted by the intensity of his strange dark gaze. "The only thing that worries me is that there doesn't seem to be very much for me to do."

"You are here to amuse my sister-in-law . . . to divert her, to handle her when her difficult moods arise. This you have accomplished very well." He took out his cigarette-case and held it towards her. "You will not be persuaded to smoke . . . Katherine?"

She shook her head. She felt confused and shy and strangely elated, because for the first time since he had asked her permission to use it, he had called her by her name. "No, thank you," she said.

He lit his own cigarette. "So you are not bored. But life is dull for you, nevertheless. Tell me, do you like—"

A shrill exclamation from the other end of the room interrupted him, and Kathy, turning her head, was startled to see his sister-in-law standing with her back to the fireplace, her eyes blazing and a fiery point of angry colour highlighting each delicate cheekbone.

"You shall not say such things!" She was speaking to the Signora, and the words seemed to be coming from between her teeth. "Vasilli was an angel—a saint! I know! For five years—for five *years*—I was married to him, and always he was so kind, so sweet, so truly good! Everybody knew it. He would have been a fine king . . . and that, too, everybody knew. Anton knew it, and he was jealous and afraid, so he caused Vasilli to be killed, and then he . . . he . . ."

"Natalia, you will say no more." Leonid had risen to his feet. His face was white, and his eyes seemed to smoulder. His voice was like the crack of a whip, and Kathy was glad it was not against her that his anger was directed at the moment.

But Natalia took no notice of him. She walked towards Kathy, and knelt down in front of her so that her blazing brown eyes were on a level with the English girl's bewildered blue ones.

"My husband was murdered . . . murdered by my brother-in-law Anton. I swear that it is true!"

Leonid looked down at her as she knelt on the brightly tinted Persian carpet, her golden skirts about her.

"You are mistaken," he said, and his voice was without any sort of expression. "You would not say such things if you were not tired. Go to bed."

There was a long pause, and then, very slowly and gracefully, Natalia rose to her feet. Her head drooped. "I . . . am sorry," she said, and her voice was a mere whisper of sound. "Truly I am sorry, Leon."

Some of the tautness vanished from the lines about her brother-in-law's mouth. "It is no matter, *petite*," he said, as gently as if the young woman in front of him had been a small and weary child. "I am sure"—half glancing at Kathy—"that nothing you have said will go beyond the walls of this room. You are upset, and," a little critically, "you have grieved too long for Vasilli."

The Princess's lip trembled. Signora Albinhieri crossed the room to take her arm, and as she did so, she threw her godson a rather curious look. "It is only a year, Leon, and some widows, you know, do not forget so quickly." She set her fingers beneath Natalia's elbow, and gently propelled her forward. "Come, *chérie*. Leon is right about one thing. You should go to bed."

Completely docile once again, Natalia allowed herself to be led towards the door, and Kathy automatically started to follow her. But then she felt the pressure of a detaining hand on her own arm, and Leonid was looking down at her.

"You are not obliged to go to bed also. The Princess's maid will attend to her."

Kathy hesitated. "But surely . . ."

At the door Natalia turned to face them, and she sent Kathy one of her sweet, abstracted smiles. "No, no, Kathy, you will stay here. *Please.* You are not to be dull because of me. I will see you in the morning, *chérie.*"

"But, madame . . ."

Signora Albinhieri interrupted her, and her voice was decisive. "It is quite all right. I myself will accompany the Princess. You have a right, Miss Grant, to an occasional undisturbed evening. It is not so, Leon?"

"Certainly it is so."

The door closed behind the two women, and for several seconds there was complete silence in the *salon.* Then Leonid spoke.

"I would prefer it if you sat down, Katherine. Are you so alarmed because you have been left alone with me? You are—what is the expression—poised for flight?"

"I—no, of course not." Blushing vividly, she sank into a deep chair, and then glanced up at the Prince. He was leaning against the mantelpiece, staring into the colourful depths of the pleasant Canaletto canal scene that hung above it, and something in his face startled Kathy. He looked drawn, and his mouth drooped wearily, and there was a quality almost of brooding sadness in the dark, velvety eyes that she had never seen in them before. She had wondered so much what he really felt about what had happened in his own country . . . whether he was distressed or perhaps, in a sense, relieved . . . whether it hurt him very much that he was now an exile and a refugee. Now she felt that she knew the answers, and she was

96

confused, because she had no right to know. The feelings that showed in his face now were too personal . . . but she could not take her eyes away from his face, and she felt such an agony of sympathy for him that tears started to her eyes, and pricked behind the lids.

And then he looked at her, and, afraid that her own feelings must have shown clearly in her face, she glanced hastily away.

"Katherine, are you fond of music?"

The question took her completely by surprise, but she was able to answer swiftly and naturally:

"Why, yes, I love it."

"Do you play the piano?"

"Only a little. I learnt while I was at school, but I haven't practised for ages."

"That is a pity. My godmother has a wonderful piano. I had hoped that you would play to me."

She lifted startled eyes to his face. "Oh, I—I'm afraid I couldn't . . . I mean, I was never very good . . ."

"Probably you are very good, but would you not like at least to see the piano? My godmother assures me that it was once used by Rossini."

She stood up, grateful for the diversion. "Yes, of course I'd love to see it."

He led the way to the door, then stood aside for her to pass through it ahead of him. They walked along a corridor, and crossed the main entrance hall. Then he pushed open another door, and they were in a handsome room a little shorter than the library. The floor here was of polished wood, scattered with vividly coloured rugs, and most of the furniture was beautiful and rather fragile, and looked as if it might belong to the period of Louis Quinze. And in one corner there was a beautiful ebony piano.

Leonid walked across to it and opened it up, revealing a keyboard only slightly yellowed with age.

"Is it not beautiful?" His long, sensitive fingers caressed the dark wood. "Would you not like to play on such a piano?"

"It's a wonderful piano, but really I'd rather not play." She looked at his transformed face, and said gently: "I expect you play yourself?"

"Yes," he said simply. His hands wandered lightly over the keyboard. "This piano knows me well . . . as I know it." He looked up and smiled faintly. "Wouldn't you even like to try it?"

"Oh, no . . . Really, I'm quite out of practice." She actually shrank back, so appalled did she feel at the thought of being obliged to display her musical skill in front of him, and she saw that he noticed the movement. "Wouldn't you . . . wouldn't you like to play yourself, *monsieur*?"

"And will you sit and listen to me?" he demanded. "Or will you run away, as I know you are longing to do?"

She coloured, but said a little stiffly: "Of course I don't want to run away. And I'd love to listen."

"Very well."

He waited until Kathy was seated on an elegant gilt-legged chair near the fireplace, and then he sat down in front of the old piano. Once again his fingers touched the faintly yellowing keys, and this time the contact seemed charged with magic. Ripples of melody that were almost agonizingly beautiful spread across the room, and Kathy, enchanted, forgot to feel uncomfortable. He had not asked her whether she had any particularly strong preferences where piano music was concerned, but he wandered from Chopin to Brahms, and from Brahms to Schumann, and almost everything he played seemed to be a favourite of hers. He seemed temporarily to have lost all awareness of the passage of time, and each liquid melody followed its predecessor after only the tiniest pause. It was as if the music provided him with a kind of safety-valve . . . an outlet for some sort of pent-up emotion, and perhaps because of this the well-known nocturnes and cantatas seemed especially wonderful and strangely disturbing. Kathy thought of all the regret and disillusionment and nostalgia that he must be feeling, and which he usually concealed so effectively, and realized that it was being given expression, perhaps for the first time, in his interpretation of Chopin and Brahms.

He ended with a softly executed Chopin nocturne, and as the last quiet notes died away Kathy realized for the first time how silent it was in the villa. It was a living, breathing silence, an extraordinary stillness, and Leonid seemed a part of it, for he remained quite motionless for several seconds after his fingers had ceased to travel over the keyboard. And Kathy remained quite still too, for the enchantment still lingered in the air like a vital, living presence, and she felt that a movement or a word would dispel it.

And then, saying nothing, Leonid slowly swung round to look at her. Her eyes were huge and luminous, and she made no attempt to conceal the wonder and admiration that shone in them.

"That was . . . marvellous!" she said, and for the first time, as she spoke to him, there was no trace of shyness in her voice.

He did not answer, but only stared at her, and in such a curious way that at last she became conscious of it, and all her pulses started to beat more rapidly. Nervously, she stood up, and began to walk towards the door.

"Thank you," she got out jerkily. "For playing to me, I mean. It was—it really was wonderful. But I think I'd better go to bed now. I must see if the Princess wants anything . . ."

Her voice trailed away as he stood up and took a step towards her.

"Please don't go," he said, and his voice was rather taut. "Not yet, Katherine."

"But I must . . ." Once again she broke off, for he had lightly taken hold of her wrist, and as a result the hand attached to that wrist had begun to tremble uncontrollably. But she had to get away . . . she *had* to get away from those suddenly limpid dark eyes that were devouring her face. She had to get away from the softly compelling voice which seemed to be tearing at something inside her. She had never felt like this before, and she was frightened. . . .

"Katherine," he said softly, "my beautiful little Katherine."

She ventured to glance up at him, and saw that he was looking at her as if she mesmerized him.

"Your eyes are like the sky at midnight," he said, "Did you know? *Katherine!*"

And then his arms were about her, and he had kissed her, quite lightly, on the lips.

For several seconds she stood absolutely still, listening to the violent, erratic pounding of her own heart, unable to think or move or speak. And then she broke away from him and dashed towards the door, blindly struggling to get it open—not even hearing Leonid's voice as he called after her, conscious of nothing but the hot tears welling into her eyes, and the knowledge that she had to get away . . . somehow.

CHAPTER SEVEN

KATHY lay awake for a long time that night, before finally managing to get to sleep, and even when weariness did overcome her, and her heavy eyelids closed, it was not for long. The slightest sound from far away in the villa had the power to disturb her, and at five o'clock, tired of struggling with insomnia, she got up and dressed. It was still quite dark, but she knew that the dawn could not be far off now, and in her present mood she felt that to sit by her window and watch the sky turning paler would be infinitely pleasanter than remaining in bed and pretending to sleep.

It was going to be necessary for her to leave the Villa Albinhieri, and with as little delay as possible. That much was clear to her. But getting herself back to England was going to require a tremendous effort of will-power on her part, and just at the moment she felt a little dazed at the prospect of attempting it. She didn't seem to be able to think too clearly . . . she was unhappy and bewildered, and tired too. She thought a little ruefully that perhaps she should at least have made sure of getting a good night's sleep, since she was going to need to be fresh and able to think for herself, and she wondered how she was going to face the day that lay ahead of her.

She was in love with Leonid. She knew that now, and supposed that if she had been prepared to admit it to herself she would have known it long ago. As far as she was concerned he was the centre of everything that made her life worthwhile, and she was quite well aware that when she had accomplished her intention of interposing some fifteen hundred miles between herself and him she would feel as if she had suddenly moved out of vivid sunlight into cold and infinitely depressing shadows. But she was not the sort of young woman with whom Leonid could ever contemplate sharing his life. That was quite obvious. When he did eventually marry, his wife would undoubtedly be chosen from amongst women of approximately his own social standing—or at least, from among women to whom attached some sort of material advantage. No doubt some such person as an American heiress would be regarded as an extremely useful addition to the family, especially as their circumstances in the future could hardly be precisely what they had been in the past.

And she, Kathy Grant, had nothing whatsoever to offer. The daughter of an English country clergyman, with scarcely a penny to her name—without even any surviving relatives to whom she could turn in an unexpected emergency—it was completely impossible that Leonid could at any time have looked upon her as the sort of girl whom he might, conceivably, honour with an offer of marriage.

And yet he had kissed her . . . and that one kiss had upset her more than anything else. As far as she was concerned, its only immediate effect had been to consolidate her feelings, revealing to her in a startling flash of realization that she loved him, and possibly had done from the first day she met him. But he did not love her—or if he did, it was not the sort of love he would be likely to bestow on a woman whom he intended to marry. Perhaps, encouraged by her schoolgirlish admiration for his skill as a pianist, he had merely been indulging—or attempting to indulge —in a light flirtation, or perhaps he had had in mind an association which would be rather more serious, though scarcely more satisfactory from her point of view. She was actually more inclined to believe that in kissing her he had merely succumbed to passing impulse, and by the morning might even have forgotten the incident, but whatever the explanation she knew that she could no longer remain in his sister-in-law's employment, and that the first thing she had to do was to explain her decision to Natalia at the earliest opportunity.

The opportunity arose shortly after breakfast, when the Princess sent her a message by one of the maids, asking her to visit her in her room.

Strong sunlight was filling the big, beautiful apartment when Kathy entered. Natalia was lying back against her lace-edged pillows, and the morning's mail, partially opened, was littered across the golden satin of her eiderdown. Tossing some of the letters aside, she cleared a space so that it was possible for Kathy to sit down on the side of the bed, and then dropped a single sheet of extremely elegant notepaper, covered in spidery feminine handwriting, into the English girl's lap.

"It's Liczak," she said, and sank back against her pillows. Temporarily distracted from the problems burdening her own mind, Kathy glanced at her, recognizing the danger signals with which she had gradually become familiar since entering the other woman's employment. The brown eyes held an appealing look, and there was a faint flush in the alabaster cheeks.

"You see what she says." One slim hand gestured towards the letter in Kathy's lap.

"It's in your language, madame; I can't read it."

"Well, she says she is coming here. Oh, Kathy, it was such a *relief* when she asked if she could stay in Paris for a while! But Leonid was not pleased, and now he will say it is good that she is to come! I don't like her, Kathy! She makes me feel miserable!"

Mechanically, Kathy smiled at her, and put the letter back amongst the mass of correspondence littering the eiderdown. "Perhaps she won't come," she suggested, knowing quite well as she spoke that if the Baroness Liczak said she was coming there was very little chance indeed of her failing to arrive.

"Of course she will come." Long lashes drooped across the lustrous brown eyes, and rather slowly, Natalia added: "She is bringing her daughter with her."

"Well . . ." Kathy wondered what she ought to say to this. "Won't that be rather nice? I mean, she must be quite young. She might be an ideal companion for you."

"I don't care what she might be. I am angry that she should be coming here. Of course, the Baronin asks permission to bring her, but naturally she would be very surprised if it were not granted." She sighed, then struggled into an upright position, and shot a rather curious look in Kathy's direction. "I think . . ." She paused, evidently pondering something. "I think I would like you to take a message to my brother-in-law for me. You will probably find him in the library. Tell him . . . just tell him that I asked you to let him know about the Baroness." Natalia seemed to smile slightly, and added: "You need not mention her daughter."

Kathy felt herself turn pale, and her pulses started hammering uncontrollably. "Madame—" She struggled for words, trying to think. "Would it be all right if I gave the message to someone . . . to one of the maids?"

"But why?" The Princess's slim eyebrows rose, and she gave Kathy a long, rather wide-eyed stare. Then she looked away, and started sorting her letters.

"No. If you do not *very* much mind, *petite*, I would prefer you to give him the message."

"But . . ." Kathy tried to think of something to say, some plausible excuse to make that might save her from the necessity of coming face to face with the Prince—a situation which she had hoped to avoid. She had hoped, in fact, that it would not be necessary for her to see the Prince again.

She hesitated on the edge of explaining everything to Natalia; but her courage failed her, and in any case it would not have been easy to mention any such delicate matter when the person in whom she wished to confide was determinedly engaged in sifting through her correspondence. So she simply stood up, and said:

"Yes . . . very well. I'll do it immediately, madame."

She had meant to let Natalia know that she had to leave . . . she had intended to tell the other woman everything; now, somehow, she couldn't do so, but she didn't know how she was going to face Leonid—even for a few seconds. Perhaps, though, she would after all be able to give the message to his secretary.

It was quite cool in the big square entrance hall when she reached it, for the morning sunshine did not penetrate to that part of the villa. Kathy started to shiver, although she knew that it was nerves rather than the chill in the air which made her do so, and as she knocked on the library door she hoped that when it was opened the unsteadiness in her tightly clasped fingers would not be too noticeable.

When the door was opened she received a shock. She had been hoping to be confronted by the thin, bespectacled features of Jasik Grun, Leonid's young Tirhanian secretary, but when the wide white door swung inwards it was a very different kind of face that looked down at her, and stood in tongue-tied immobility, while a painful flush mounted to her cheeks, and her eyes were instinctively lowered.

As her eyes *were* lowered, she didn't see the troubled look in the Prince's dark ones as they gazed at her. But she did hear his voice. He said:

"Good morning. I am glad you have come to see me." His voice was soft, and curiously grave.

Some of the agonizing colour deserted her face, and she ventured to look up at him.

"The Princess Natalia sent me . . . with a message. I am to tell you that the Baroness Liczak will soon be arriving from Paris."

There was a pause. Then in a rather curious tone Leonid said: "I see. My sister-in-law felt that I ought to know that?"

"Y-yes." Kathy felt confused again, and twisted her hands together. "She thought—she thought you would be pleased."

"Ah, yes—well, I expect it will be a good thing."
He stopped, his eyes studying her face. "Katherine,
come and talk to me," he said abruptly.

She started. "Oh, but I must—I think I should go
back . . ." she began.

He glanced down at her with a trace of a smile.
"Is Natalia waiting for you?"

"No, but—"

"I have something to say to you . . . Please listen
to me. Just for a few minutes, Katherine."

She swallowed. "Well, I—"

He put his head on one side, and surveyed her
thoughtfully." I promise you, you will be perfectly
safe."

"Yes, of course! I—I didn't mean . . ." She broke
off, blushing furiously. "Naturally, if there is anything you would like to say to me—"

"Well, there is . . . and I don't want to postpone
it, Katherine."

He ushered her into the room, and closed the door.
She stood still, a little way inside the room, looking
distinctly uneasy, and very much as if she were
poised for instant flight. Her blue eyes were very
wide, and there were tell-tale shadows underneath
them which showed quite plainly how little she had
slept the night before.

"Won't you sit down?" He gestured towards one
of the huge leather armchairs.

"No, I . . . I'd rather stand by the window. It's
such a lovely morning. It doesn't seem like December, does it? I mean, not an English December. But
of course, this isn't England. It's Italy."

"Yes, it's Italy." He followed her over to the
window, and glanced over her shoulder at the sunlit

gardens of the villa. "Do you feel . . . strange here, Katherine? Bewildered? Homesick?"

"No, I've been perfectly happy here," she told him truthfully, and wished he would not stand so close to her. Why couldn't he say what he had to say, and let her go? He fumbled with his cigarette-case, as if he intended to smoke; but then he apparently changed his mind, and returned it to his pocket unopened.

"Katherine," he said suddenly, "if I ask you something will you give me an honest answer?"

"Yes, of course. Of course, *monsieur*."

"Why did you run away last night, after I had kissed you?"

Once again she flushed painfully and to conceal the fact moved closer to the window.

"Surely," she said in a muffled voice, "it was obvious why I ran away."

"You were alarmed . . . shocked, perhaps?" She wondered if he could be making fun of her, but he sounded perfectly serious—even anxious. "You were angry with me?"

For a moment or two Kathy couldn't bring herself to say anything at all. And then, somehow she seemed to discover a new composure, and her voice was almost detached as she said:

"It was the music, the atmosphere—everything, I expect. You were . . . carried away."

He was silent. He was silent, in fact, for such a long time that she began to feel embarrassed again. Why did he go on torturing her like this? He had evidently asked her into the library in order to satisfy his curiosity concerning the odd mentality of a foolish little English girl who upset herself over a

109

casual kiss. The interview had gone on quite long enough, and as she didn't think she could stand very much more of it it seemed to her that the only thing to do was to bring it to an end as quickly as possible.

"There is no need to apologize," she said—rather drily, for it didn't seem to her that he had any intention of apologizing, or even that he saw any necessity to do so. Not that she wanted an apology— she knew very well what she wanted, but also knew that the less she thought about it the better.

Suddenly determined, she turned briskly to face him, and as she did so she saw that he was staring at her as if there were something about her that bewildered him. Before she could move any further, he put both his hands on her shoulders, and looked down into her face.

"Did you say . . . Katherine, do you believe that— that last night I was *carried away* by the music?"

She lowered her eyes. "Well . . . well, I suppose— it was very emotional music, wasn't it?"

He drew a deep breath. "And I am a lonely, exiled prince, and you are a pretty little beggar-maid?" Strange little sparks appeared at the back of his dark eyes, and his fingers gripped her shoulders more tightly. "Tell me, is the attraction purely temporary, do you think? It might be . . . but of course, it might also last for quite a while—perhaps as long as a month! I am not absolutely sure how long it is usual for such an attachment to last . . . it will be necessary for you to tell me. You see, Mademoiselle Katherine, I have been wasting my opportunities. Obviously it is expected of me that I should flirt with young women . . . it is my—what is the word?—prerogative! It is distressing to think how many have probably been disappointed. But, you understand, I had the strange idea that, should I attempt to make love to such a young woman as yourself, that young woman would in all probability assume me to be *in* love with her. And as I have never before been in love, I have accordingly never before made advances to such a young woman as yourself!"

Kathy stared at him. Her legs were trembling slightly, and she was trying to sort out what he had been saying—to bring it into focus in her mind. She had the vague impression that, despite all the anger and sarcasm in his voice, he was trying to say something absolutely wonderful. But she didn't believe it. It didn't make sense—it couldn't make sense . . .

And then she heard the soft hiss of tyres on the gravel driveway beneath the window, and the whisper of an excellent engine subsiding into silence. At first she didn't pay very much attention to either of these sounds, but gradually she became aware that Leonid was paying attention to them, that, in fact, his attention was being completely distracted by something he could see below him in that open space where the car would have stopped. She had her back to the window now, but he could see through it easily, and so completely absorbed did he appear to be in whatever or whoever it was that had just arrived outside that at last she turned her head and followed the direction of his eyes.

A large grey Mercedes had come to a standstill outside the main door of the villa, and while a smart, uniformed chauffeur bent over the contents of the boot, the three people who had just alighted from the car sauntered slowly towards the steps which led up to the front door of the house. One was a man, some-where about forty years of age, tall and distinguished and vaguely military-looking, but it was the two women, one of them rather more than middle-aged and the other young, who caught Kathy's eyes.

For the elder of the two was the Baroness Liczak, and the younger was one of the most striking women she had ever beheld in the entire course of her life.

She was not, perhaps, strictly speaking, as beautiful as Natalia, whose fragile, golden, un-sophisticated looks really were remarkable; but there was a kind of poise, a flawless elegance about the slim figure of the girl now slowly mounting the steps to the main entrance that would turn a good many heads at any gathering, and for no obvious reason Kathy felt an extraordinary chill as she looked at her. Sleek, shining dark hair and smooth, pale skin; a cream-coloured silk suit that bore the hallmark of Paris . . . She and the Baroness were talking now, to someone who had met them in the doorway, and Kathy could hear the younger woman's soft, at-tractive laugh, and then her light, rather husky voice as she spoke to someone in fluent Italian.

Leonid's hands had dropped from Kathy's shoulders, and he turned away from her into the room. Kathy stood still, feeling bewildered and curiously deflated, like someone who has been abruptly awakened from a happy dream. She was silent, for she couldn't, in the circumstances, think of anything to say, and she was still feeling rather dazed, for she hadn't any idea why the dream had been disturbed.

But Leonid had walked coolly over to a big desk at the far end of the room, and had started to sift through some papers, evidently looking for something. To her astonishment, he suddenly looked up and glanced at her, rather as if she were something that had temporarily escaped his memory.

"Katherine," he said, "we will talk later. You do not mind?"

"Of course not." Kathy's voice was small and tight and stiff, and it hurt her, rather as it had hurt her once when she had laryngitis. "I'll tell Her Highness that the Baroness has arrived."

"Yes, it will be best for you to do so. And mention also that she is accompanied by her daughter, and by my friend, Colonel Zanin."

The Baroness's daughter! Well, the Baroness could justifiably be proud of her. Not only was she extremely lovely, but she had the power to make Leonid of Tirhania drop everything as soon as he caught sight of her—even when he was in the middle of conducting a flirtation with his sister-in-law's English secretary!

As soon as Kathy had delivered the Prince's message to Natalia, she retired to her own bedroom, pleading as an excuse that ever since the night before she had been suffering from a slight headache. Natalia was very sympathetic, promising to make all the necessary excuses on her behalf when she failed to put in an appearance at lunch, and pressing on the English girl some pills which she assured her were excellent for headaches.

"You will lie down all the afternoon, and then by dinner-time you will be well again, and ready to join us downstairs. I am sorry that you cannot be with us at lunch, for Liczak is so much easier to bear when you are there, but you must not worry about that, *chérie*." She gave Kathy rather a curious look. "What did Leon say when you told him about Liczak? Of course, he did not know that she was going to arrive so quickly!"

"He said he expected it would be a good thing," Kathy told her, remembering his words without the slightest difficulty, just as she seemed to remember everything he had ever said to her.

"He's a tyrant," said Natalia lightly. But her eyes narrowed as she studied Kathy's small white face, and with more perception than she was usually given credit for recognized the tension in the clouded blue eyes. "Go and lie down, *chérie*," she repeated. "And this evening I think we will have a little talk, you and I."

But before Kathy had had a chance to have any 'little talk' with her employer, their mutual hostess, Signora Albinhieri, elected to pay her a visit. It was about five o'clock when she tapped lightly on Kathy's door, and the rest of the villa was fairly quiet. Kathy had been sitting in an armchair, staring through her window at the broad, distinctive top of an umbrella pine-tree, but when the *signora* entered the room she stood up rather hastily, and in an attempt to conceal the fact that she had been idly brooding, picked up the novel which had been lying beside her on a small table.

"My dear!" The *signora* smiled at her, her peculiarly sharp dark eyes seeming to take in every detail of her appearance. "Forgive me for intruding upon you, but when I heard that you were not very well I felt that I should make an effort to find out whether you were comfortable."

"Oh, I—I'm very comfortable, thank you *signora*," assured Kathy rather hastily, wishing that the old eyes were not quite so penetrating. "And as a matter of fact, I'm not really unwell. I . . . just had a bit of a headache. It was very kind of the Princess Natalia not to insist upon my being present at lunch."

The old lady looked a little amused. "Yes, you should not under-estimate the extent of the sacrifice she made. You are a great support to her, and she is so frightened, poor child, of Elena Liczak. A married woman, and the sister-in-law of the King—the ex-King—" rather drily, "of Tirhania, and she is terrified of that woman! She is such a *bambina*, that one . . . it is incredible."

Not being quite sure whether or not it would be strictly ethical for her to join in this discussion of her employer's peculiarities, Kathy smiled a little uncertainly, and then suddenly remembered her manners and urged the *signora* to take a seat, indicating the luxuriously comfortable arm-chair which she herself had been occupying. The old lady accepted the invitation, and lowered her unsubstantial frame into the chair with an effortless dignity which Kathy could imagine being instilled into her years ago in Tirhania, when she was still a very young girl, and her life was ruled by stern and unrelenting governesses.

Then Kathy also sat down, and the *signora's* bright eyes began to study her again.

"Tell me, child, you are acquainted with Elena Liczak?"

"Yes; she was with the Princess when I first met her, in London."

"She is a hard woman . . . I don't suppose you like her?"

Rather taken aback, Kathy hesitated. "She's a difficult person to know," she remarked, conscious of the fact that she was being evasive.

The *signora* looked as if this reply afforded her some considerable amusement. "Not *difficult* to know," she murmured. "You probably know her as well as you ever would know her. The truth is, *petite*, that there is little more to her than you have already seen, I daresay. There is no sentiment, no warmth in her nature. But she is ambitious." There was a pause. "Her daughter," continued the *signora* deliberately, "is almost certain to become the wife of my godson Leonid."

Kathy looked at her quite steadily, but her eyes were very darkly blue, and rather hollow. "I . . . see," she said.

"Do you?" The other's voice was gentle, but Kathy had the feeling that there was a hint of steel about it as well. "Do you really see? Do you understand, Katherine Grant, that your loving him so much won't make him love you . . . certainly won't make him marry you?"

Kathy's face flamed. "I didn't know—" she began. "I mean," she said simply, "I didn't realize that it was—so obvious."

"Love, even one-sided love, such as yours, has an uncomfortable habit of becoming obvious . . . especially," with a small, not unsympathetic smile, "to interfering old women like me. Listen, my child," watching the girl's expression closely, "Leon was born to fulfil a certain role in life. That role may have changed now, but it is hard for a man of thirty to turn his back on everything that has been important to him since his early childhood. I do not suggest, *cara*, that he is a man in love with his own dignity, but he is a prince of Tirhania. It is a fine thing to be a prince of Tirhania, but it also involves leading a life of service. Leon cannot forget what he is—he wishes to serve his people. Perhaps—I do not know —he dreams of leading them, as his father and grandfather did before him—as his brother, Anton," with a soft sigh, "does not know how to do. He is not a man, child, who could fade into obscurity." She glanced piercingly at Kathy. "If he did so, he would die."

Kathy was about to speak, but, with a gesture, the old lady prevented her. "For the moment," she said, "he must wait. He must bide his time, as you say in England. But the day may come . . . He has an aim to work for, and nothing must interfere with it. Nothing must be allowed to interfere with it. And when he marries, his wife must be entirely suitable. No newspaper columnist—" with a biting edge to her voice—"must ever be in a position to criticize her conduct . . . or her background."

Kathy bit her lip, and when she spoke her voice was husky, and strained, and barely recognizable.

"You need not worry, *signora*. Naturally, the Prince couldn't marry me—even if he were in love with me, which of course he isn't. And I—I wouldn't do anything that would hurt him. But I think that I ought to go home to England—as soon as possible. If you could help me explain . . . to Natalia . . ."

At this stage her voice gave way completely. She struggled valiantly with the lump in her throat, and the hot, stinging moisture behind her eyelids, but her

117

self-control was nearly exhausted, and the tears began to cascade down her cheeks like rain.

Signora Albinhieri leant forward and took one of her hands. "Child, don't cry . . . don't cry."

She didn't seem to be capable of saying very much else now, and Kathy wished with all her heart that the small, autocratic figure whose bony fingers were grasping hers like a kind of chilly vice would go, and leave her alone. She knew what she had to do . . . it wouldn't even be necessary for her to think about it. It was what she had intended to do, really, ever since the night before, when she had run away and left Leonid alone in the *signora's* music-room. She had to admit to herself that until now, despite everything, she had been conscious of a faint, barely acknowledged feeling of hope—although she really didn't know what she had been hoping for—but now she felt ashamed of that hope, for she saw quite plainly, more plainly, in fact, than she ever had before, how tremendous the gulf between her and Leonid really was. And she saw that even if Leonid himself had wanted to bridge that gulf—and he did not—she could not have allowed him to do so, for to attempt to bridge it would do him irreparable harm.

Her tears ceased, and she blew her nose, saying in a rather blurred voice: "I'm sorry, *signora.* I didn't . . . intend to cry."

"Well, it is a good thing to cry, they say, when one has a great sorrow."

There was a silence so complete that Kathy could hear the birds singing in the orange-trees outside, and then the *signora* slowly levered herself out of the big armchair. Kathy rose also, and they stood facing one another, while the last rays of a rather pale wintery sun slanted through the windows, glinting on the older woman's rings and the girl's chestnut hair.

"If you wish, I will speak to Natalia." The *signora's* voice was calm and matter-of-fact.

"Thank you, but I think I would prefer to—to speak to her myself."

"Then I will say *addio* to you, and leave you to become calm again." One of the thin hands touched Kathy's shoulder. "You *will* forget . . . in time, you will forget. Everything is forgotten in time."

When she had gone, Kathy wandered over to the window, and stood looking out. Despite the fact that this was Italy, and the Mediterranean lay less than a quarter of a mile away, the sky looked cold and rather menacing now that the sun had slipped below the horizon, and heavy grey clouds were building up behind the umbrella pines. She remembered that in England, too, the skies would be grey—in fact, the weather would probably be very bad indeed. She wondered how she would feel when she found herself once again resident in her own country, and how easy or otherwise it would be for her to get another job. She didn't want to trade upon the fact that she had been employed by the Karanskas . . . But she had some rather excellent qualifications in any case, and if she went to a good agency it shouldn't be too difficult. She started to think about the journey home. Since arriving in Italy she had spent little or nothing of her salary, and she should be able to pay her own way back to England. She would go over-land, of course—that should be much cheaper than travelling by air. And she still had a small sum of money in the bank at home; enough to tide her over until she did succeed in securing a new job.

She let her mind dwell for a long time on the practical details of getting home; it was so much safer than dwelling on other things.

Just before six o'clock she made up her mind to go to Natalia's room, and tell her employer everything without any further delay. Natalia had said they must have a little talk—she wondered, briefly, what had been meant by that—and somehow she thought the other girl would understand how she felt, better perhaps, than anybody else. Whatever Natalia's failings and weakness might be, she could be very kind, and she was sensitive—to others feelings, as well as her own.

But just as Kathy was about to leave her room, she was temporarily halted by the sudden arrival of Natalia's maid, who had been entrusted with an urgent request for the English girl to visit her mistress immediately. The maid did not speak very much English, but her eyes were sparkling like stars, and she radiated a kind of suppressed excitement.

When Kathy reached the Princess's room, her employer was standing in front of a wide open wardrobe, and there was a dress over her arm. It was a white dress with a long, trailing skirt, and it had the unmistakable shimmer of pure, expensive silk. It was an evening dress, and as Kathy stood in the doorway watching, Natalia held it up against herself, and executed a half pirouette in front of one of the mirrors lining the wardrobe doors. Then, as she turned, she caught sight of Kathy, and almost seemed to dance towards her.

"*Chérie*, do you like this dress? I bought it in Paris, and people always say that white suits me well, and yet—do you think that perhaps black . . . or the grey chiffon? As I am a widow, and a—what is the word?—an exile, and I want to do what is *convenable*, of course."

She was still holding the dress against herself, and laughing like an excited child, but as Kathy stood still, saying nothing, it seemed to occur to her that her present behaviour was probably a little mystifying to the other girl.

"But you do not know!" she exclaimed, throwing the dress on to a chair, from whence it was promptly rescued by the maid. "You don't know why I sent for you, do you? You cannot imagine, *petite*, what a beautiful surprise I have for you!"

Whatever the surprise might be, Kathy found it very difficult to believe that it could have the power to bestow any pleasure upon herself, but she forced an automatic smile to her lips. This was not the moment . . .

"We are to go to the opera!"

"The opera?" Kathy's voice was blank.

"Yes. It is all decided. We are not to be shut up in this place any longer. Leon says that we have to appear in public some time, and apparently there has not been a reporter outside the gate for two whole days! They will not worry us now, and besides, we have to face people. So Leon has reserved a box at the opera-house in Genoa, and we are to go there tonight! Isn't it exciting, Kathy? It was not easy to get the box, I think, at such short notice, but of course when the manager knew who it was for . . .

Nobody else knows that we are going; it will be quite a surprise for everyone!"

That would certainly be true. Kathy had a vision of journalists and cameramen from all corners of the globe jostling one another for a brief glimpse of the fascinating Tirhanian exiles; and she wondered whether Natalia realized that such an outing might turn out to be rather exhausting—even upsetting. Still, since Leonid had planned it . . .

Quietly, she asked: "Who will be going with you, madame?"

"Why, you, of course, *chérie*, and Leon . . ." She wrinkled her nose slightly. "And Sonja Liczak, I suppose. But," with more enthusiasm, "her mother, the Baronin, will not be coming." She added casually: "Colonel Zanin will be with us. He is Leon's friend from the Embassy in Paris, you know."

"Yes, I know. But, Madame . . ." Kathy tried to think how best to say what she wanted to say, "I'd rather not—I mean, is it absolutely necessary that I should go with you tonight?" She didn't want to spoil Natalia's pleasure in the opera by going into the question of her own problems now—they could be sorted out in the morning, much as she would have preferred to have everything settled as soon as possible. But she didn't think that at the moment she could face the prospect of such an evening as Natalia was envisaging—and in the company of Leonid! "You will have Mademoiselle Liczak with you, and in any case, I—I wouldn't fit in."

"*You* would not fit *in*?" For a moment the other girl stared at her in wide-eyed amazement, and then she laughed, and caught hold of Kathy's sleeve.

"Don't be modest, *mon amie*, it is silly, and not at all helpful. You will wear your beautiful blue dress— you remember, the one you bought in Paris?—and Sonja Liczak and I will be quite . . . quite . . ."

"Overshadowed?" suggested Kathy, with a faint tinge of wry humour. "I shouldn't think so. Your Highness, I was born and brought up in a country vicarage in England, and I'm not used to—well, to attending magnificent functions with . . . with people like yourself."

"You should not say such things. Really, I am surprised." The mild brown eyes looked quite severe. "Your poor father was a man of the Church, and could not have been more respectable . . . you have told me. Why should not his daughter go to the opera with anyone? It is wicked, I think, to be ashamed of your family."

Kathy attempted to explain that she was not in the least ashamed of her family, but she could not prevent Natalia from reading her a brief but rather astonishing lecture on the subject of the inferiority complex with which, it seemed, she was supposed to be afflicted. She remembered the headache from which she had claimed to be suffering earlier in the day, and wondered whether that might possibly save her from the necessity of joining in the evening's entertainment, but then, suddenly, she wondered why she was struggling so hard to avoid this outing. Certainly, it would be a strain . . . it would probably be embarrassing. But arguing with Natalia was also a strain, and if she did go to the opera it might not be so very bad. If Leonid were escorting the dazzling Sonja Liczak he would be unlikely to spare so much as a glance at her, and with any luck she would be able to remain entirely in the background. She loved music, and perhaps, after all, it would be more bearable than spending the evening alone in her room, with nothing but her highly unsatisfactory thoughts for company, or going to bed early, and struggling vainly to get to sleep.

She would not admit to herself that, if she did want to go, it was probably because she might never again have an opportunity to be with Leonid.

CHAPTER EIGHT

IT was an important night for the Opera House in Genoa, for it was to be the first night of a new operatic season, and for at least a week past every seat in the building had been booked for this opening performance. It had only been with the greatest difficulty, and much discreet manoeuvering, that the manager had been able to secure a box for the use of the former Tirhanian royal family, but under no circumstances would he have turned them away—one did not turn such people away, and something could always be managed. There would be tremendous excitement, of course, when it dawned on the general public that they were present, and with the practised skill of one long accustomed to the entertainment of celebrities he made discreet arrangements for the handling of the Press, and anyone else who might display an interest in the royal party. Of course, he could not prevent the possibility of something of an uproar being caused, at least outside the building . . . He hoped Their Serene Highnesses realized the sort of thing they might be called upon to face.

At precisely five minutes to eight, a handsome white Jaguar slid smoothly into the Piazza di Ferrari, and drew noiselessly to a halt outside the Opera House. It was the same car in which Kathy had travelled from the airport to the Villa Albinhieri more than three weeks before, and as she once again shared the luxuriously upholstered rear seat with her employer she couldn't help pondering on the difference between the state of her emotions now and her feelings on that earlier night.

Then, she had been smarting beneath the knowledge that the Prince was angry with her—in fact, she had fully expected to be sent home to England the following day. She had been upset; but she had also been tired, and everything had seemed a little blurred. Perhaps, also, she had known that Leonid would never dismiss her ... not as summarily as that. Leonid was essentially kind. The thought brought an embarrassing mist into her eyes, and as she determinedly stared through the offside window the brilliant street lights of Genoa seemed to quiver hazily in front of her.

It had been decided that she, Natalia and Colonel Zanin should travel in the Jaguar, and that Leonid should accompany Mademoiselle Sonja Liczak in the grey Mercedes which had brought her from the airport earlier that day, and was the property of Signora Albinhieri. Kathy was glad that the *signora* was not accompanying them, but was staying at home to spend a quiet evening with the mother of Sonja Liczak—however much she might dislike her—and she was also glad that so far Leonid, at least, had paid very little attention to her.

At least, she succeeded in convincing herself that she was glad.

Natalia had been distressed because when she came to think about it she realized that Kathy was, in a sense, going to be something of an odd one out in the party. That three ladies should be escorted to an important evening function by only two gentlemen was, in her eyes, not at all a satisfactory arrangement, and even she understood perfectly well that the Princess Natalia and Sonja Liczak must be considered the most important of the three women. But at length Kathy had succeeded in convincing her that she was not in the least offended by the arrangement, and had even brought her to see, after a time, that it would be much pleasanter for her to be able to give her attention wholly to the music. She assured her employer that she would very much dislike on such an occasion to have had a particular escort assigned to herself, and although Natalia patently had difficulty in comprehending this viewpoint she eventually appeared moderately satisfied, and observed that she and Kathy would be able to amuse themselves by commenting on the appearance of any other female opera-goers who came within their line of vision.

Leonid and Sonja Liczak had arrived at the Opera House just ahead of the remainder of their party, and the manager was just bowing them over the threshold when the Jaguar crept silently to the foot of the steps. There were more bows for Natalia, and even for Kathy and the aristocratic-looking Colonel Zanin, and then they were all climbing a handsome staircase, attended by the manager, and Kathy realized that any other late arrivals who felt curiosity about them were being kept, discreetly, at a distance.

There were plenty of admiring glances for Natalia, ethereally regal in the floating white silk, but, although Kathy did not realize it, there were even more cast in her own direction, as she slowly climbed the stairs a little behind her employer. She was wearing the midnight blue evening gown which, under Natalia's supervision, she had purchased in Paris, and she herself knew, as she had known when she first tried it on during that hectic shopping expedition in the French capital, that nothing could have suited her better. Her hair, which she had washed the day before, shone like polished chestnuts in the soft light from the chandeliers, and at Natalia's suggestion, the Princess's own maid had arranged it for her, sweeping it up into a glorious gleaming coil which drew subtle attention to the delicate contours of her small oval face. Her eyes looked huge, and very deeply, startlingly blue, but only someone who knew her very well would have noticed the shadows lingering in their depths.

Leonid and Sonja Liczak had already been shown into the reserved box, for it had not been considered desirable for them to attract curiosity by lingering in the foyer, and when the rest of their party entered they were standing near the door, well out of sight of the vast, murmurous concourse of opera-goers assembled far below them in the packed auditorium. Occupants of some of the other boxes possibly had a view of them, but so far they had attracted no attention, for Leonid, at least, was almost in shadow, and his female companion had so positioned herself that her own slender, exquisitely clad form was interposed between the interesting exile and the eyes of the inquisitive.

It was the first time Kathy had really had an opportunity to study at close quarters the woman who, she was assured, was to become Leonid's wife, for Mademoiselle Liczak had kept the remainder of the party waiting for perhaps two minutes before they left the Villa, and by the time she made her appearance in the doorway Kathy had already been installed in the Jaguar. So now the necessary introduction was made, and Kathy felt the fingers of her right hand taken in the lightest possible hold, while a pair of beautiful but cool grey eyes surveyed her with what might possibly have been a slightly startled expression behind them, and the merest suggestion of a not very enthusiastic smile touched the pink, delicately moulded mouth of Sonja Liczak. She was wearing an extremely elegant creation of silver-grey lace, topped by a slim evening coat of the same material, and as her gloves and her small satin slippers were the colour of pearls, she resembled a kind of symphony in grey. Only her gleaming, jet-black hair, coiled into an elegant pleat at the back of her head, and that small pink mouth, provided anything in the nature of an effective contrast. But the overall effect was undeniably effective, and there was little doubt that she knew it, for after the one brief moment in which she had seemed to register something like surprise at the appearance of the English girl her lovely face resumed what was probably its habitual expression of mild complacency, and as she turned back to her princely escort there was a smile lurking at the back of her eyes which indicated that in her opinion he, at least, could have little interest in the charms of other women while she was present.

It was also necessary for Colonel Zanin to be introduced to Kathy, and as she looked into the Colonel's kind, rather handsome face, and felt her hand taken in a firm, reassuring clasp, she felt herself relax a little. At least there was one member of the party, apart from Natalia, who did not fill her with disturbing sensations of confusion or resentment. And she could not help resenting Sonja Liczak, try as

129

she would to tell herself that the other girl was exactly the right sort of wife for Leonid, and that in any case it was no concern of hers what sort of wife he selected for himself. An uncomfortable lump arose in her throat every time she permitted herself to think about the interview she had had with Leonid only that morning, and the moment when it had seemed as if the wonderful shining dream, which she scarcely dared admit to herself she had ever cherished, might be about to come true. Now, of course, she realized that, for Leonid's own sake, she could not have allowed it to come true, but just for that one marvellous moment anything and everything had been possible . . .

And now she knew that he had, after all, merely been amusing himself—or perhaps it was just that he was a little weak where such matters were concerned?—and as soon as the woman he intended to marry descended from her car at the door he had realized that the time had come to bring the interlude to a close. Or, at least, to put such entertainments aside for a while.

Tonight he was startlingly good-looking in full evening dress, and as he had even donned orders and decorations, and his bearing was suddenly, subtly more autocratic than usual, he seemed to Kathy remote and magnificent and a little strange. But her heart ached, nevertheless, as she looked at him, and she knew that whatever guise he appeared in he would always have the power to make her feel that her life was not really worth very much if it were not to be lived in company with him.

When he caught sight of her he simply accorded her a small bow, and a smile that as a greeting to his

130

sister-in-law's paid companion could not have been more appropriate. She had not really expected anything more, and confined her acknowledgement to an inclination of the head and a small, formal smile, but this demonstration of his indifference only served to rub salt into the wounds which had already been inflicted on her that day, and she felt slightly sick.

They were moving into the front of the box, for the overture was about to begin, and a vague stirring and whispering around and below them betrayed the fact that they had been recognized. The whispering grew into a noticeable hum, as heads were turned, and hundreds of eyes became focused on the royal box, and the conductor of the orchestra became plainly agitated. Those dedicated music-lovers who had come to hear an opera, and simply wished to give all their attention to that opera, were beginning to regard their more inquisitive neighbours with disfavour, and several upraised voices were to be heard requesting silence.

With unruffled composure, almost as if they had not noticed the effect which had been produced by their appearance, Natalia and Leonid took their seats, and Sonja Liczak and the Colonel followed their example. In the surrounding boxes, opera-glasses which had been raised and focused with unnerving deliberation were slowly lowered; and, in the auditorium, comment and speculation began to subside, and eyes were reluctantly turned back to face the curtained stage.

Kathy marvelled at the skill with which her employer and the Prince had handled the situation; she was sure that it was their calm, their very indifference, that had quietened those curious tongues so

131

rapidly, and while from Leonid she would have expected little else, she was surprised that Natalia could, when it was necessary, appear so startlingly poised. She sensed that the ordeal, from their point of view, was as yet far from being over, but for the moment every voice in the building was hushed, for the Overture was about to commence.

The opera being performed was *Rigoletto*, and Kathy was glad, for, at least from the musical point of view, it was her favourite. Only once in her life had she been privileged to visit Covent Garden—on the evening of her sixteenth birthday, in the company of her father and a young girl cousin—but ever since her schooldays she had adored the work of the great Italian composers, and she realized that whatever else this evening might be, it was a musical treat of no mean order. Her seat was in a corner of the box, slightly apart from the others, and as the curtain rose upon Renaissance Italy she closed her eyes and prepared to lose herself in the majestic, melodious depths of Verdi's masterpiece.

An hour later, feeling dazed, exalted, and rather out of contact with the world around her, she realized that the interval had arrived. The huge building was once again ablaze with lights, and everywhere there was movement. Colonel Zanin was bending over her, politely enquiring what she would like in the way of refreshment, and Leonid had also risen, and was standing behind Sonja Liczak's chair. One of his hands was lightly resting on the dark girl's shoulder, and as Kathy glanced at them she thought, with a sudden sharp pang, that they were a strikingly well matched pair. Her pleasure in the music was forgotten in the cold misery which washed over her like a tidal wave, and Colonel Zanin, waiting patiently to discover her tastes in liquid refreshment, was at last obliged to repeat his enquiry.

Recalled abruptly to herself, she looked up at him apologetically, and he smiled.

"You were far away, *mademoiselle?* In ancient Mantua, perhaps?"

"No—that is, yes. It's a wonderful performance, isn't it?"

"Enchanting. One finds it difficult—don't you think?—to bring oneself down to earth again."

But she had the uncomfortable feeling that he had followed the direction of her eyes, and that he was feeling more than a little sorry for her because the undeniably romantic figure of his friend had so obviously inspired in her a hopeless, schoolgirlish infatuation. An infatuation so uncontrolled that she could not refrain from casting jealous glances in the direction of any other woman he spoke to, even if the woman happened to be his fiancée—or almost his fiancée.

Feeling, suddenly, that she had to get away from them all, if only for a few minutes, she asked the Colonel to procure her the nearest possible thing to a straight lemonade, and then as he turned away from she her picked up her tiny, silvery evening bag, and slipped out into the softly-lit corridor beyond the door of the box.

Immediately she felt better, for the air, for some reason, seemed cooler in the corridor, and for a moment she stood quite still, savouring the sudden solitude, and the knowledge that she was, temporarily at least, out of reach of prying eyes.

And then she realized that she was not, after all, quite alone. Footsteps were advancing towards her along the corridor, and, as they drew nearer, they were slowing down.

"Pardonnez-moi, mademoiselle!"

She turned her head, and found herself face to face with a tall, sandy-haired young man, whose appearance, it seemed to her, was unmistakably English. His blue eyes brightened perceptibly as they took in all the details of her own appearance, and he smiled rather engagingly. He also looked as if something had suddenly dawned on him.

"Isn't it Miss Grant . . . Miss Katherine Grant?"

"Yes . . . yes, that's right."

"Well, that's lucky. They said you might be able to help me." He grinned. "And it's always good to see a compatriot in a place like this."

Her eyebrows puckered a little, and she stared at him rather blankly. She wasn't in the mood for light conversation, and it was beyond her to imagine in what way she could be of assistance to him. But she waited politely for him to continue.

He had the grace to look very slightly embarrassed. "It's just that I have to know the name of the other lady in Prince Leonid's box. Apart from you and the Princess Natalia, that is. She . . ." He hesitated, as if uncertain whether he ought to continue, and then added conspiratorially: "She's his fiancée, I believe."

Afterwards, Kathy could not imagine why she answered him . . . why she told him anything at all. But at the time it seemed to her that he didn't need to be told very much. Obviously, she thought, he knew for a fact that the strange young woman in the

134

Prince's box was the Prince's prospective wife, and all he needed to discover was her name . . . possibly in order to have some message conveyed to her. The very manner in which he spoke—as if the matter were extremely confidential, and only to be discussed with such privileged members of the entourage as herself— seemed to her to indicate that he was a reliable person who had received his information in confidence, but in a perfectly legitimate manner.

"She is Mademoiselle Sonja Liczak," she told him, and even in her own ears her voice sounded oddly flat. "I could take a message to her, if you like."

"No, thanks very much, but . . . The engagement will be announced pretty soon, I expect?"

"Yes, I expect so." There was a kind of controlled eagerness in the young man's face which puzzled her, and suddenly she felt vaguely disturbed.

But he evidently had all the information he wanted. "Thanks again," he said, smiling at her quite dazzlingly. "I just wanted the name—for a friend." A minute or two later he was gone, striding away briskly down the wide, crimson-carpeted corridor, and Kathy was left staring after him, and feeling very slightly troubled.

But she didn't have time to feel troubled for very long, for suddenly the door of the box swung open, and Natalia emerged, on her way to repair her makeup in the powder-room. She had just seen a dress in one of the other boxes for the privilege of owning which she would apparently be prepared to make quite a few sacrifices, and as she laid a hand on Kathy's arm and drew the English girl along with her she began to describe it in considerable detail. There didn't seem much point in mentioning the young

Englishman to her, and in any case there wasn't a great deal of opportunity. When she had finished with the subject of the dress she began to talk about Colonel Zanin, and Kathy gathered that she was more than a little attracted by her brother-in-law's closest friend. It had been noticeable all evening that the Colonel, for his part, found it difficult to take his eyes off Natalia's delicate profile, while her pale, swinging hair and general air of helpless fragility quite obviously fascinated him. The fact that he was the same Colonel Zanin whose escort she had fled Paris to escape seemed to trouble neither of them. Now that she had met him, Natalia found it rather amusing to recall the lengths to which she had gone to avoid having such a delightful man as a travelling companion, and he himself clearly thought that her fears had been entirely comprehensible, and her method of reacting to them endearing rather than anything else. He was a bachelor, and came from an excellent family, and there seemed little doubt that before very long he and Natalia would be announcing the fact that they intended to get married.

Probably, thought Kathy dully, there would be a double wedding in the Karanska family, which would be nice for the newspapers.

She and Natalia returned to their box, where the other three had been awaiting them, and once again, as they all sat down, she drew her own chair very slightly aside, so that she was not obliged to talk to anyone. Colonel Zanin handed her the long, cool, sparkling drink she had requested, and she realized that, had he not been completely dazzled by the charms of one of the other young women present, he would not have allowed her to retire so completely into herself, for he was essentially polite and kind. But he was utterly under the spell of the princess, and Kathy was glad of it, for she didn't think that, that evening, she could have managed to maintain a flow of light, normal conversation for any length of time.

Leonid had taken absolutely no notice of her—in fact, he was behaving as if she didn't exist—and although in some ways this made things easier for her, it hardly did anything to lift her spirits. Although she knew so well that she could never mean anything in his life, it was hurtful to be shown that he could ignore her so completely—even his fiancée could scarcely object to his addressing one or two casual remarks to the English girl who was only there to attend upon his sister-in-law.

Once again the lights in the vast auditorium were dimmed, and the curtain slowly rose upon the second half of the famous opera. But by now she was developing a slight headache, and the music she usually loved seemed harsh and discordant. The story of *Rigoletto*, too, to which she had never previously paid a great deal of attention, now began to strike her as peculiarly repellent. She felt ridiculously nauseated by the spectacle of poor Gilda's pathetic devotion to her somewhat unsavoury duke, and as she couldn't help dwelling on the fact that there seemed to be several points of resemblance between the fictitious villain and Prince Leonid it was perhaps not surprising that she soon began to wish the performance would end.

And then, at last, it had ended, and for fully ten minutes the entire Opera House seemed to reverberate with the full-throated approval of a gratified Italian audience. The *prima donna*, who had certainly been excellent, was showered with bouquets and smaller floral tributes from all corners of the building, and she took numberless curtain calls, while the shouts of *"brava"* grew, if anything, more and more persistent, and Kathy felt that if she had to stand very much more of it she would scream. Her temples throbbed and ached almost intolerably, and she was terribly tired . . .

Natalia turned and looked at her, and instantly her eyes registered concern. "Kathy, *chérie*, you are very pale . . . It is the heat in this place. But when we are outside you will feel better." She herself was looking rather radiant, and it occurred to Kathy that she had never seen her employer looking like that before. Of course, the unexpectedness of this evening out, after her spell in seclusion, had done a lot to cheer her up, but it was perfectly obvious that Colonel Zanin, still watching her in a hypnotized fashion, had done even more, and Kathy could not repress a small sigh. For some people, everything was so easy . . .

They left their box before the applause had really begun to die away, in the hope that by doing so they might be able to slip out of the building almost unnoticed, but this small stratagem was doomed to failure. Their departure had been watched for and duly noted, and by the time they reached the foyer it was packed. As they descended the stairs a sea of faces was turned upwards to watch them, and camera flashbulbs exploded in all directions. The manager and his staff cleared a path for them with commendable speed, but just for a few moments they were actually brought to a standstill, and it was a little frightening. Kathy saw Sonja Liczak swallow quite noticeably, and turn pale, as the human mass surged around the foot of the staircase on which they stood, and then she glanced at Leonid, and realized, with a little shock that set all her pulses racing, that he was looking straight at her, Kathy. For an instant their eyes met, and she forgot all about the jostling crowd below, and even the photographers' lights. Then he looked away, and as he did she saw that the people in the foyer were gradually being forced apart to let them through.

Outside, in the Piazza, the night air was startlingly cool and refreshing, and although the more persistent of the journalists and cameramen followed them out on to the steps their cars were waiting for them, and in almost no time they were being driven smoothly and almost silently away from the hectic scene at the entrance to the Opera House.

When they arrived back at the Villa, Kathy prepared to follow Natalia up to her room, but the other girl took a long, keen look at her pale, oddly strained face and ordered her to go to bed immediately.

"You had a headache this afternoon, didn't you? I forgot—I'm so sorry, *petite!*" She looked thoughtful. "And we were going to have a little talk . . . But," more briskly, "we will have it in the morning, I think, for tonight you are *fatiguée,* and so am I."

Alone in her own bedroom, Kathy sank down on the stool in front of her dressing-table, and stared at her reflection in the huge crystal mirror which confronted her. She was very pale, and her eyes were enormous and shadowed, their natural hue darkened by the depth and intensity of the colour in her dress. Slowly, she unfastened the single row of pearls, a bequest from her grandmother, which had been her

139

only adornment that evening, and she put them away quite methodically in the case in which she had always kept them. After that, she supposed she ought to be thinking about getting undressed, but somehow she didn't seem to have the energy. The sooner she went to bed, the sooner the morning would come; and in the morning she would have to tell Natalia that she could stay with her no longer. Natalia was helpful and sympathetic—Kathy could not help wondering how much she had guessed, lately, about the English girl's thoughts and feelings —but there would be nothing that she could do, except help her unhappy employee to return to her own country as swiftly as possible, and that was probably precisely what she would do.

By this time the following evening she might easily be in London and Leonid would have gone out of her life for ever.

She lifted a hand to her head, and was just about to start uncoiling her hair when there was a tap on her door, and Rosa came in, looking distinctly apologetic.

"*Scusa, signorina*, but the Signor Principe would like to talk to you."

Kathy stared at her, while her pulses began to race. Lenoid wanted to talk to her . . . ?

Her mouth felt dry, and her legs trembled uncontrollably as she walked along the corridor and across the hall to the library—the same library in which she had fainted on her first night in the Villa; the same library in which, that very morning, she and Leonid had begun to discuss something that just for a few moments it had seemed might be important to them both.

140

And Leonid had said: "We will talk later." Was that why he had sent for her now?

But as soon as, in response to a somewhat harsh 'Come in', she had pushed open the door and entered the room, she knew that the man standing with his back to the marble mantelpiece was in anything but an amiable humour, and at the look on his face something inside her turned cold. He executed a small, stiff, continental-style bow, and indicated a chair.

"You will please sit down, Miss Grant."

It was a long time since he had called her 'Miss Grant', but even without the abandonment of her Christian name his voice would have told her that he was very angry—and, apparently, with her.

She made no attempt to linger by the door, but with a curious detached dignity walked slowly across the room, and obediently sank into the red leather chair.

His eyes followed her, and as she looked up at him the expression in their inky depths was quite unfathomable.

Then he turned away from her, and lit a cigarette. "I have just received a telephone call," he told her. "From London." He exhaled a puff of smoke, and appeared to be studying the tips of his sensitive, well cared for fingers. "It came from the editor of a newspaper called the *Daily Courier*. I was surprised, but I cannot imagine, *mademoiselle*, that you would have been." He shot a swift glance at her, and went on: "I had not intended to announce my engagement yet, but obviously it was your opinion that the world should not be kept in ignorance any longer."

She gasped, and every vestige of colour remaining in her cheeks deserted them.

141

Leonid looked at her, and his eyes were cold and black and unrelenting. "Apparently the *Daily Courier* had a representative at the opera this evening. But of course, you must know that. You very kindly granted him an interview, and the information which you gave him was so interesting that he naturally telephoned his head office at the earliest possible opportunity. He was quite a young man, evidently, and inexperienced. They had not expected him to 'come up', as his editor phrases it, with such a valuable story."

"Oh!" said Kathy, and the colour came back into her face in a revealing tide of crimson. "I didn't think —I didn't know—that he was a reporter . . ." At first, she had scarcely understood what the Prince was saying; it had seemed to her that someone must have made a serious mistake. And then she had recollected the sandy-haired young Englishman who had spoken to her in the corridor, and she realized with painful clarity that she had indeed made a grave mistake. "I thought . . ." she began again, and then her voice trailed away, and she abandoned any attempt to make excuses for herself. She had done an unforgivable thing; she had betrayed all the confidence that had been placed in her, and in an unthinking moment had blithely given vital information to a man who she now realized had had all the appearance of a typical journalist.

"Whatever you may, or may not, have thought, Miss Grant," said Leonid unpleasantly, "you certainly seem to have been very definite in what you said to the gentleman from the *Daily Courier*. He told his editor that he was quite sure there could be no mistake. He had spoken to someone who was in a

142

position to know the truth—Miss Katherine Grant, Princess Natalia's English secretary."

"I'm sorry," Kathy whispered, and looked down at her own tightly clenched fingers.

"Well, I am glad that you are sorry." His accent was much more noticeable than it usually was, and Kathy thought that never before had he seemed so alien and frightening. "My sister-in-law has been good to you, I believe—very good! She has treated you as a member of her own family, and I should have thought that to her, at least, you would have wished to be loyal. I, of course, have incurred your resentment." His lips tightened, and he looked straight at her. "I thought you very pretty, *mademoiselle*—I still think you very pretty!—and unfortunately, as you realized, I have a weakness for pretty young women. I have to pay them some sort of attention! That did not please you, and no doubt you are quite pleased to have been responsible for placing me in a fairly embarrassing position."

Kathy looked up at him. "Oh, no, I—"

He interrupted her. "Perhaps you do not think it an embarrassing position? Well, it is only embarrassing because Mademoiselle Liczak did not wish the announcement to be made quite so soon, but it was a little annoying to be obliged to explain the situation to a total stranger at this hour of the night!"

"I—I'm sorry, Your Highness," she said again, and stood up. Almost every word he had spoken had pierced her like the blade of a sharp knife. She couldn't think very clearly any more; but she did know one thing, and that was that she had to get away from the Villa Albinhieri within the next few hours. He *was* going to marry Sonja Liczak; he had

143

only shown an interest in her because he had a weakness for 'pretty young women'; and she wished with all her heart that she had never even seen Ransome's hotel, for if she had never been a receptionist there she would never have met the cold-blooded arrogant man who was now staring down at her disdainfully from his position in front of the great grey marble fireplace.

"I . . . think I'd like to go to bed now," she told him, wishing that she could stop the curious shivering sensation deep down inside her. And she added: "I'll leave early in the morning. I'm sure Her—Her Serene Highness will agree that that is the best thing." She didn't know how she was going to manage it, but she would arrange things somehow.

"My chauffeur will drive you to the airport." He wasn't looking at her, and with a numb feeling of shock she realized that he had no intention of suggesting that she didn't need to leave quite so abruptly. Probably if she hadn't suggested that she leave in the morning he would have done so himself!

Just as she was about to open the door and escape, he spoke again. "I imagine I have your permission to convey your apologies to Mademoiselle Liczak? I feel strongly that you owe her an apology!"

"Yes, of course. And do tell her that I . . . ope she'll be very happy—*when* you decide to announce your engagement!"

She left the room swiftly, with her head held high . . . but as soon as the door had closed behind her her shoulders began to droop as if beneath an insupportable burden, and it was all that she could do to get herself back to the temporary sanctuary of her own bedroom.

CHAPTER NINE

THE following morning was wet and cold—for Italy exceptionally cold—and Kathy awoke heavy-eyed, and with a severe headache. But she knew exactly what she had to do, and as soon as she had consumed a cup of coffee—which was as much as she felt she could face in the way of breakfast—she lifted the receiver from the smart white telephone beside her bed, and contacted the British Consulate in Mirano. She asked if it would be possible to speak to Mr. Robert Markham, and in no time at all she was rewarded by hearing the reassuring, essentially English accents of the young man who had visited her shortly after she arrived in Italy.

"Miss Grant!" He sounded positively eager. "I've been making all sorts of attempts to get in touch with you—I called at the Villa twice, but the first time I called the maid told me you were out, and on the second occasion she said you just didn't want to see anybody. I thought it seemed pretty odd, actually, and I tried to get you on the telephone, but that didn't work, either. They haven't been holding you prisoner in there, have they?"

Kathy laughed, as he probably expected her to do, but it didn't really strike her as being at all funny. She had known nothing about Robert Markham's visits, or his telephone calls, and she wondered on whose instructions she had been kept in ignorance of them. It didn't matter very much now, as it happened, but it was strange—and irritating.

Nevertheless, for his benefit she thought up a reasonably plausible explanation which seemed to satisfy him, and then got down to the real reason for her getting in touch with him. He listened in silence, and then said, with quick sympathy:

"Something must have gone rather badly wrong for you to want to leave so suddenly—if you don't mind me saying so, you sound as if you've had just about enough. But you don't have to tell me anything about it if you don't want to. Look, at a guess I'd say you don't want to have to ask any of the Karanskas for transport to the airport, do you?"

Her throat constricting, Kathy admitted that she didn't. "But I don't even know how to find a taxi, you see . . . if you could tell me where I could get one . . ."

"You don't have to worry about a taxi." His voice was brisk. "I'll run you over to the airport myself, and then I can help you get your flight fixed up. It might not be easy to get a seat at such short notice, but I'd probably be able to arrange it for you."

"Thank you." She was genuinely grateful. "It's terribly kind of you."

"Well, I told you you could always rely on me, and to tell you the truth I've been worrying about you a good deal lately. I'd a feeling you might be needing help . . ." There was no reply, and after a moment he went on: "There's a flight leaving Genoa for London at about lunchtime. Could you make it in time, do you think? It would mean my picking you up at about twelve o'clock." As there was still no answer from the other end, he spoke rather more sharply. "Are you there, Miss Grant?"

"Yes . . . yes, I'm here." He thought that her voice sounded rather muffled; and decided that it was probably a bad line. "I'll be ready at twelve o'clock." Thinking swiftly, she added: "I'll walk down to the main gate."

"Well, if you'd rather . . . but are you sure? I mean, won't you have a fair amount of luggage?"

"No—no, I won't have very much luggage." She would arrive back in London with the clothes she had already possessed when she left London. Nothing on earth would persuade her to take any of the things she had bought with money paid her by the Karanskas. "And thank you," she said again. "I didn't intend to put you to so much trouble—I just thought you might be able to advise me."

"Well, if you want some advice I'll do my best to give it to you . . . when I see you. But don't worry about your journey home. I'll see to that."

After that, the morning seemed to pass very swiftly. She packed the one and only suitcase she intended to take with her, and then sat alone in her room, and waited. During the night, while she had lain awake, tossing and turning, for hours, she had decided that she couldn't possibly face a farewell, explanatory interview with Natalia. As soon as she got back to England she would write her—but she couldn't talk to her now. Fortunately, the Princess had given orders to the effect that she was not to be disturbed until noon, and by the time she felt able even to sit up and sip a cup of coffee Kathy would probably be well on her way to Genoa airport.

She had been rather afraid that at any moment she might receive a message from the Prince, informing her that he, or his secretary, had made arrangements for her flight home, and although she was relieved when no such message came, she was also surprised. Leonid, she knew, had such a strong sense of duty . . . she had always felt that, whatever happened, he would always be considerate. Especially to insignificant female employees upon whom he could scarcely find it worthwhile to vent his anger.

But she had obviously offended him seriously—so seriously that he did not even intend to offer her any assistance where the question of her journey home was concerned . . . despite the fact that the night before he had said: "My chauffeur will drive you to the airport!"

At exactly twenty minutes to twelve, she picked up her suitcase, and took a last look around the bedroom she had occupied for the last three weeks. On the dressing-table she had left a note for Natalia, and one for her hostess, Signora Albinhieri, and she had also left a wad of travellers' cheques, securely encased in a separate sealed envelope. They represented what was left of the advance salary she had received—quite a considerable amount—and she was heartily thankful that so much of it had been left untouched. At least she owed them nothing. She was leaving without giving formal notice to Natalia, but at least she had not robbed anybody of anything, and before she even reached London the Princess would know why she had left, and would probably feel that it had been the only course open to her.

She managed to slip out of the house completely unobserved—which was fortunate, since she didn't quite know what she would have said if she had encountered anyone—and it occurred to her, as she stepped out into the rain and erected the light umbrella which she was taking with her, that this was the second time since she became involved with the Karanska family that she had set forth on a journey in a stealthy and secretive manner.

She proceeded down the drive at a fairly brisk pace, and by the time she arrived at the main gates it was still not quite twelve o'clock. As she stood waiting, rain dripped relentlessly on to her shoulders from the branches of the tall, dark cypresses guarding the entrance, and every so often she glanced nervously back along the winding, tree-shaded drive, half expecting to see the white Jaguar or the grey Mercedes come creeping soundlessly towards her—perhaps with Leonid or even Natalia inside.

But there was no movement from the direction of the Villa. Kathy began to shiver, and to wish that she had not been quite so determined to be on time, and not keep Robert Markham waiting. The road which ran past the gates was probably one of the busiest in Italy, and as she stood there heavy traffic roared past her in an unending stream. There were sports cars and buses, articulated lorries and even oil tankers, all apparently trying to get somewhere in the shortest possible space of time, and when the slightest hold-up was occasioned there arose from dozens of assorted motor-hooters the most ear-splitting cacophony of protesting sound that Kathy had ever heard in her life. The air was heavy with the nauseating smell of petrol fumes, and in addition to being cold and wet and decidedly miserable, she began to feel slightly sick.

And then, quite suddenly, a very smart white sports car detached itself skilfully from the stream of north-bound traffic, and slipped inside the open Villa gates, to come to a standstill beside the forlorn figure of Kathy.

"I say, I'm sorry." As he spoke Robert Markham jumped out of the car, and took Kathy's suitcase from her. "You must have been waiting for ten minutes—I daresay you're soaked to the skin. But I got held up a mile or so back . . . Get into the car." He held the nearside door open for her, and surveyed her in a worried fashion as she climbed inside. "You're sure you wouldn't like to slip back to the house and change? We've a forty-minute drive ahead of us, and you must be feeling like a drowned rat—"

"No, thank you." Kathy shook her head. "I'm perfectly all right. I stood under the trees, and escaped the worst of it."

"You escaped the worst of it!" He grinned at her as he let in the clutch, and started to execute a cautious turn. "You're wet through, and I'm really awfully sorry to have kept you hanging about like that."

They slid through the gates, and paused for just a few moments on the edge of the busy coast road. And then, as soon as an opportunity arose, they joined the frightening line of traffic, and were off on their way to Genoa. Robert Markham bent down and switched on the heater, then looked sideways at Kathy with a touch of curiosity.

"I've booked you a seat on the plane," he told her. "You'll be back in London by six o'clock this evening."

"Thank you," she said gratefully. "It's . . . really awfully kind of you." She added uncomfortably: "I oughtn't to let you help me like this."

He smiled at her. "My dear, you could say it's my job. I'm at the Consulate, and you're a British subject . . . a British subject in need of assistance. Not that this sort of thing is exactly part of the regular service, of course, but you're rather a special case. And in any case, you're not at all the sort of girl who should be alone and unprotected in a foreign country!"

She smiled, and made an effort to look reasonably light-hearted, since she felt that the least she could do in the circumstances was to be a fairly amusing travelling-companion; and in any case, she didn't want the Englishman beside her to guess at her unhappiness. If he did, he might begin to speculate about the causes that lay behind it, and since his grey eyes had the appearance of being decidedly shrewd he would probably make quite an accurate guess.

He drove very fast, at times alarmingly fast, and it took considerably less than the forty minutes he had allowed to get them to the handsome modern airport at which Kathy and the Princess Natalia had landed—unexpectedly—three weeks earlier. She paid for her ticket, and he went with her into the departure lounge. By the time she had spent some ten minutes in the cloakroom, attending to her appearance, she looked considerably less bedraggled, but her bright hair, confined beneath a cream-coloured silk scarf, was still a little damp, and her small black court shoes were spattered with mud.

Robert Markham, however, thought that she could hardly have looked more attractive, as she lay back in a deep armchair, and looked up at him with a rather wan little smile. The only thing about her that worried him was the fact that the smile *was* so wan, and that her small face looked so alarmingly white. He didn't know why she was running away from the Karanskas—he hadn't asked her, and he didn't intend to do so, although he had an uneasy feeling that she was badly in need of advice—but whatever the reason it was causing her a great deal of unhappiness, and he didn't like to see it. Apart from anything else she was one of the most fascinating little things he had ever seen, with her huge violet eyes and her glorious hair, and he found himself wishing with profound and unaccustomed vehemence, that she had been staying in Italy a little longer—or at least that he had been more successful in his various attempts to see something of her while she was in Italy. Of course, she was going home to England, and he, too, would be going home some time . . . But the Katherine Grants of this world didn't usually remain unattached for very long, and there might even be someone waiting for her. Somehow, he didn't think that he would stand very much of a chance . . .

A little after one o'clock her flight was called, and she stood up and held out her gloved right hand to him. He gripped it very firmly, and she wished he would not look so searchingly into her face.

"Thank you . . . thank you very, very much," she said, smiling at him as warmly as she could. "You've been so—"

"Kind to you. Yes, I know . . . you said so! But what I've really been doing, you know, is pleasing myself." She blushed faintly, and he laughed. "Have a good trip, and if ever you're in Italy again . . . well, get in touch with me."

It was still raining quite hard as she crossed the tarmac, but in no time at all she was mounting the steps of the aircraft, and then a smiling stewardess was relieving her of her umbrella and showing her to her seat beside a comfortable, middle-aged American matron. The atmosphere was warm, and oddly peaceful, and the American matron beamed at her as they both fastened their seat belts.

Despite the rather poor weather conditions, they made a very smooth take-off, and although for most of the way they were flying through dense cloud the journey was remarkably uneventful. Kathy accepted a pile of glossy magazines from the stewardess, and pretended to become absorbed in them, although in actual fact for most of the time she scarcely saw the pages before her eyes. The American woman at her side turned out to be of a sociable disposition, but fortunately she derived considerably more pleasure from talking than from listening, and it was entirely unnecessary for Kathy to contribute more than an occasional monosyllable to the conversation. She heard about the other's fairly extensive travels described in great detail—Venice, Rome, the Greek islands and the Yugoslavian coast filling in the time until they touched down in Paris, and the glories of Andalusia and the north coast of Africa colouring the final stage between Paris and London. When they parted at the Customs barrier, the older woman pressed her hand as if they had known one another for some considerable time, and before she was forced to turn away bestowed a curious smile on Kathy.

"I don't really know what's troubling you, honey, but I could make a guess . . . And my advice is, forget him!" Then she smiled again, and was swallowed up in the huge concourse of incoming travellers.

Feeling startled, disconcerted, and more than a little annoyed with herself, Kathy got herself through Customs and passport control, and then boarded a bus which was headed for London.

She had laid her plans before leaving Italy, and she knew exactly what she was going to do. There was a girls' hostel in Central London at which she had known she could be reasonably certain of obtaining accommodation—just to set her mind at rest on that point she had telephoned the hostel immediately after her arrival at the airport—and she would stay there for a few days, while she looked around for a job. She hadn't a great deal of money left, but she had enough to keep herself for a month or two if it should be necessary—provided, of course, that she wasn't at all extravagant. And she had every hope that she would be able to find a job in a very much shorter space of time than a month.

In London it was very cold, and rain was falling with depressing persistence from a sullen grey sky. She supposed that she should at least feel some sort of relief at being home, but she didn't; she simply felt a strange sense of numbness, and a complete inability to do more, at the moment, than plan for her immediate future.

Very early the following morning she set out to do a round of the employment agencies, and by lunch-time, to her considerable astonishment, she was already in possession of a job . . . the position of private secretary to a director of one of London's most important estate agencies. It was a job which called for efficiency, a good appearance and a pleasant manner; and the shrewd-looking grey-haired woman who interviewed Kathy seemed to feel that she represented the embodiment of these virtues. On the next morning she started work, and within a week she was fairly well settled in . . . although there was still something about her which her employer, a benevolent but not usually particularly perceptive elderly man, frequently found puzzling. He wouldn't have expected her, as a responsible, hard-working young woman, to bubble over with an unceasing flow of high spirits, but it seemed to him that her attractive mouth had a curious droop to it; and then there was the lack-lustre expression that stole into her eyes whenever she imagined she wasn't being watched. He was extremely pleased with her work, into which she appeared to be throwing herself with an almost unnatural zest, but he hoped that there wasn't anything too serious on her mind, and he suggested to her that she might indulge in rather more recreation than he fancied she had been indulging in just lately. A day in the country, he told her, would do her all the good in the world, and she nodded and smiled politely, and said that she'd probably try it. But she had no intention of doing anything of the kind, for leisure meant having time to think, and that was the last thing she dared to do. She avoided thinking of anything at all that could have a connection with her own personal life, and she was heartily thankful that, generally speaking, her new job was a demanding one and left her little time during the day to consider her own affairs, even if she had wanted to consider them. And at night she was too tired to think, and after a makeshift supper went straight to bed.

Her first weekend was spent wandering disconsolately round a selection of art galleries which she had imagined might divert her, and in attending Sunday morning service at St. Martin's in the Fields—after which she felt slightly more cheerful—and when she arrived back at her desk on the following Monday morning she stared at the work which lay in front of her, and wondered how she was going to get through it.

By mid-morning she felt very little better, and when she was told, by means of the intercom, that an extremely important client wished to see Mr. Hartley, her employer, she sighed rather heavily, because every small effort seemed a little too much for her just then.

When she contacted Mr. Hartley, in his inner office, she discovered that he was in the middle of a very important long-distance telephone call, and could not see any client, however important, for at least another five minutes, so she gave instructions for the gentleman to be shown into her office instead, and wearily but instinctively patted her hair and brushed a tiny speck off the otherwise immaculate sleeve of her plain blue dress.

When the door opened, she did not look up immediately; she had just caught sight of what looked to her like an absurd mistake in a letter she had just finished typing, and her eyes were still lingering on the error when somebody spoke . . . and she decided that either she had slipped into a kind of day-dream, or her ears were playing tricks on her.

"Good morning, Miss Grant," said the voice. "How strange to find you here."

She lifted her eyes, and an odd little shudder ran through her. "Your Highness!"

Leonid carefully closed the door behind him, and then walked across to the desk. "This coincidence is really quite extraordinary, *mademoiselle*." He paused, and looked down at her. "How are you?"

"I'm . . . all right, thank you."

"My sister received your letter. I believe she has replied to it."

"H-has she?"

He glanced around him in an almost bored fashion. "May I sit down? Your employer, I believe, will not be able to see me immediately."

"No." She swallowed, and bit her lip in an effort to stop it trembling. "Then . . . you do—"

"I do wish to see your employer? Yes, of course. Charming as this unexpected encounter is, it *is* unexpected. I did not know, *mademoiselle*, that when I entered this room I would see you sitting behind that desk. How could I?"

She realized that he was waiting for her to resume her seat before sitting down himself, and she slowly sank back into her chair, at the same time, with tremendous determination, forcing herself to look straight at him.

In a small, tight, muffled voice, she said: "I hope the Princess—well, that she understood why I left so . . . suddenly."

"I am sure she did." He smiled, but his eyes were abstracted, and she had the impression that, beyond being mildly surprised at seeing her where she was, he was not in the least interested in her. "I am looking," he told her suddenly, "for a house in England.

157

Do you think that your . . . Mr. Hartley, is it not? . . . will be able to find me something suitable?"

Kathy stared at him. "A house . . . in England?"

"Yes. As, you understand, I am being married so soon. And I think my wife and I will definitely wish to settle in England."

"I see." To her, it seemed absurd to continue the conversation, but as he evidently wished to behave as if he were an ordinary customer who had never seen her before today she moistened her dry lips and made a violent effort to talk in a normal matter.

"What—what sort of house are you looking for?"

"Oh, an old house . . . I think. Yes, I am sure, an old house. I don't think that my future wife would appreciate a modern one. Quite large, of course . . . Not too large, but it is important to have accommodation for one's friends. A family house—I believe that is the correct expression?"

The intercom buzzed on Kathy's desk, and she was spared the necessity of answering him. Her employer could see him now.

He bowed to her as he got up, and once again, before he entered the inner office, bestowed on her that slight, detached little smile.

Twenty minutes later he emerged, with Mr. Hartley at his elbow, and both men looked more than satisfied with the results of their discussion. Leonid executed another small bow in Kathy's direction, and Mr. Hartley beamed at her.

"Put those papers aside, my dear. You're going down to Sussex for the day!" He smiled at her again, and added, not without a rather quizzical expression in his keen brown eyes: "I had no idea that you and Prince Leonid were known to each other!"

To her annoyance, Kathy felt herself blushing. "Yes, we—we met a short time ago." She had always felt guilty because she had not told her present employer about the very last job she had occupied, and she felt more so now. She could not meet Leonid's eyes, but she knew instinctively that he would not have told Mr. Hartley any details of their acquaintanceship. He must think it rather odd, she supposed, that she should not have mentioned having held a position which any young woman would be proud to have occupied. He could not know that it hurt her even to remember, in the private recesses of her own mind, that she had once lived under the same roof as himself. "G-going down to Sussex?" she repeated, as she suddenly realized the implications of what had just been said. "You want me to . . . go down to Sussex?"

"Yes. I shan't find it very easy to spare you, I'll admit, but the Prince was insistent." He looked at Leonid almost indulgently. Clients of his calibre did not appear every day, even in the offices of London's topmost estate agent. "His Highness is interested in Chanbury Manor; you may remember I discussed it with you. It's near Little Chanbury, and that's not terribly far from Chichester. Anyway, it's in West Sussex. It's a fairly long journey, but the Prince has a car with him, I understand. If you leave now, you should get to Little Chanbury by early afternoon— stopping for lunch on the way, of course." He looked affably from one to the other of them, and Kathy realized with embarrassment that he had decided they might not be particularly anxious to hurry. If Leonid had insisted upon detaching her from her regular duties so that she should be free to give him her personal attention perhaps his assumption was not entirely incomprehensible, and only Kathy knew that in doing such a thing the Prince could only have wanted to hurt her in some way.

She could not really understand it—she would never have believed him to be quite so mercilessly vindictive—but she supposed he felt that his revenge was not yet entirely complete. An afternoon of polite but cruel taunting—was that what lay in store for her?

But there was no possible escape, and in any case she knew—although the knowledge made her despise herself heartily—that she didn't really want to escape. An afternoon in Leonid's company . . . He might taunt her, he might be quite brutal, but she would be with him. She would sit beside him while he drove, she would hear his voice—speaking to *her*— and only this morning she had expected never to see him again . . . It was like being granted a reprieve, and although it was only a temporary reprieve, and the whole purpose of the excursion was the inspection of a house which he would one day share with Sonja Liczak—when, of course, she was no longer a Liczak! —she couldn't do anything about the light which sprang into her eyes as she looked at Mr. Hartley, and which only he saw.

"I . . . I ought to go home and change," she said, glancing down at the dark blue dress.

Leonid nodded briskly. "I'll drive you." He held open the door, at the same time bestowing a formal smile on Mr. Hartley, and then followed Kathy out of the room and down the stairs to where a smart pale blue sports car was waiting by the kerb. She looked at him a little apprehensively as he placed her

160

in the passenger seat and then settled himself behind the wheel, but his face was completely impassive, and he said nothing whatsoever until he brought the car to a standstill outside the hostel in which—largely because she couldn't be bothered to move—she was still sharing a cheap room. Then he said:

"This is a hostel for young women?"

"Yes." He was looking distinctly disapproving as he helped her to alight, and she glanced at him in surprise. "I have to stay somewhere," she said a little stiffly, "and this sort of place is rather convenient. And it's inexpensive too, of course."

"But you have a very good job, I think?"

He sounded as if he were determined to get to the bottom of the matter, and Kathy felt a little confused. It didn't occur to her to think his pointed questioning impertinent, but she hesitated for a moment before answering slowly: "I suppose I just haven't bothered . . . to look for anything else . . ."

"I see." Something in his voice made her look quickly and instinctively up at him, but the expression in his eyes was utterly unreadable. Then he closed the car door with a snap, and said briskly: "Don't be too long. I can't park here for more than ten minutes."

Just over seven minutes later she returned, this time wearing a light tweed suit ornamented with a very attractive golden fleck, and a pair of slim, elegant, casual shoes. In her hand she carried a folded silk headscarf, just in case it should become necessary to protect her hair against the elements, but as a pale, early spring sun was just on the point of emerging from behind the clouds, and the temperature was decidedly warmer than it had been in

England for weeks past, it seemed very likely that she might not be needing the protection.

Leonid started the car, and for twenty minutes they weaved and threaded their way through the intricacies of London streets and London traffic, then they were in the suburbs, moving along broad streets lined with houses, and Kathy sat staring in front of her, and wondered why the man at her side was so obviously determined not to speak . . . and why, in fact, he had wanted her with him at all.

By the time they reached the green, open country, it was nearly noon, and the day had begun to fulfil its earlier promise of being bright and comparatively warm. They sped through the small, picture postcard villages of Surrey, and every so often the road wound through bare, grey woods—in which this morning, for all their bareness, there was a strange feeling of awakening life.

Still Leonid did not speak to her, but, despite his silence, and the fact that this would probably be the last time she would ever see him, Kathy felt almost happy. She could look sideways and see Leonid's chiselled features . . . the slight frown contorting his brow as he concentrated on the curves of the road ahead. And she could study—discreetly, of course— the deep waves in his thick, dark hair, and watch the way in which his capable, sensitive hands controlled the swing of the steering-wheel.

It wasn't very long before they had crossed the border into Sussex, and just a little after half past one they stopped for lunch in Midhurst. The inn which they decided to patronize was very old, and very lavishly equipped, and the food was excellent, but Kathy wasn't particularly hungry, and Leonid seemed detached and almost impatient. She realized that he was anxious to see the house which he might, by the end of the afternoon, be intending to buy, and because she didn't want to hold him up any longer than was strictly necessary she hurried through her own lunch, and refused coffee. He looked faintly conscience-stricken as he handed her back into the car, and when he had got in himself he looked at her.

"You did not have a good lunch. I hurried you too much."

"It was a very nice lunch, and I didn't feel at all hurried," she assured him, without very much truth, but with an absurd desire to set his mind at rest. "How soon do you think we shall get to Little Chanbury?"

"In about an hour. Are you tired?" looking at her sharply, as if he had quite suddenly recollected that he was in some degree responsible for her well-being.

"Oh, no, I'm not at all tired." She sounded almost anxious. "It's—it's such a pleasant drive." For something to say, she added: "You must be looking forward to seeing the house."

He turned his head a little. "Are you looking forward to seeing it?"

"Well, I . . ." For some reason she felt confused. "I'm not going to buy it—I shan't be living there."

"Even so, all women are interested in houses, are they not?" His eyes were on the road, but he smiled slightly. "They enjoy looking for the possibilities . . . imagining exactly what sort of colour-scheme would suit some particular room, inspecting sinks and water-heaters, and old-fashioned stoves. I hope you *are* interested in all these things, *mademoiselle*," the smile becoming more pronounced, "for I don't propose to concern myself with them."

"But . . ." She looked rather agitated. "I don't know enough about things like that to—well, to give you an opinion . . ."

"But you will know if you like the house." With faultless precision, he negotiated a dangerous right-hand bend.

"It doesn't matter whether I like the house," she said rather flatly.

"Of course it matters . . . since it is you who will make the decision."

"I . . . ?" She stared at him uncomprehendingly.

"Yes, you. If there is anything about the place that seriously offends me I shall not, of course, buy it, but I intend to be guided largely by you."

She looked at him gravely, consideringly. "I . . . I don't understand," she said. "You were very annoyed with me, you dismissed me from my post—"

"I did not dismiss you. You told me that you intended to leave—'early in the morning', if you recall."

"But you *were* very angry. And yet now you—you want me to advise you on the choice of a house just as if . . . just as if . . ."

"Just as if you yourself were my fiancée?"

She looked away from him. "Just as if I were a—a family friend, instead of an employee—a former employee."

"Well, does it worry you?" He was concentrating hard on the road winding ahead of them. "Remember you work for an estate agent now. This is your job, in a sense."

"But you need not have chosen me. I mean, Mr. Hartley himself would have gone with you, I'm sure."

"You sound as if that would have been a very great honour. However," with an odd little smile, "I didn't ask Mr. Hartley. I asked you. And I assure you," flashing white teeth at her, "that I haven't brought you down here in order to exact a terrible revenge!"

Kathy said nothing.

Half an hour later they entered the village of Little Chanbury, and Leonid slowed the car to a crawl. They passed the church, a beautiful building of Sussex stone, with a tall, tapering spire, and they passed a row of thatched and weather-boarded cottages, before finally coming to rest outside the Rose and Dragon Hotel, where Leonid hailed a plump and sturdy countrywoman and asked the way to Little Chanbury Manor. The Manor, it turned out, was hardly any distance from the centre of the village, and less than three minutes later they were turning in through a well-worn gateway, and following the winding progress of a rutted and tree-lined drive.

Then they caught sight of the house, and Kathy gave a little gasp of pure pleasure, while Leonid stopped the car, and climbed out.

Chanbury Manor had been built during the sixteenth century, in accordance with the personal wishes of the man who intended to live in it. and the most skilful craftsmanship available had gone into the joining of its ancient timbers, and the placing of its small, rosy bricks. It was L-shaped, and its twin roof-trees were uneven, its tiles old and red and lichened. There seemed to be dozens of windows, all latticed and all gleaming in the pale afternoon sunlight, and there were clusters of tall, slender Tudor chimneys. All around lay its gardens, and as Kathy got out of the car she could see that there were snow-drops beneath the trees.

Leonid looked at her. "You are impressed?" he enquired.

"It's . . . beautiful." Her eyes shone with sheer appreciation, and she glanced up at him quite un-selfconsciously. "Don't you think so?"

He didn't give her a direct answer, but merely said: "Shall we look at the gardens first, or would you like to go inside?"

"The gardens are wonderful, but I'm longing to see inside," she confessed, and he felt in his pocket for the key.

"Very well. I think, by the way, that it would be as well to be prepared for rather a shock when we do see the inside. The outward appearance of a house like this is often a good deal finer than the interior."

But they did not receive any shock, for the house had been maintained in excellent order, and as soon as they crossed the threshold Kathy knew that it was the most perfect house she had ever seen in her life. They wandered through big, airy, oak-beamed rooms that overlooked the sunlit gardens, they climbed a polished staircase which would have caused any expert on Tudor workmanship to tremble with delight, and when finally they returned to the long panelled drawing-room Kathy was full of almost breathless appreciation. She walked across to one of the wide windows, and stood gazing out across the velvety lawn, while Leonid stood in the centre of the room and watched her.

"It's a wonderful room," she said, and there was a little catch in her voice.

Leonid moved towards her. "You think its future mistress will like it?"

Outside in the gardens the sunlight seemed to dim, and Kathy felt as if someone had touched her with cold fingers.

"I'm quite sure that Mademoiselle Liczak will... love it," she said, and started to turn away from the window. She was aware that he was standing quite close to her, and the fact unnerved her. "Isn't it getting late?"

"I don't think I mentioned Mademoiselle Liczak." He had placed a hand on her arm to detain her, and the sound of his voice startled her, for there was a note in it which she had never heard before. She looked up at him, all her pulses beginning to beat a great deal too rapidly for comfort, and she knew that she couldn't move ... couldn't make the effort to break away and move out of the room, out of the house, and demand to be driven back to London. "Katherine ..." His hand moved to her left shoulder, and he gave her a little shake. "Don't you understand ... ? Why do you think I wanted you to come with me? Don't you *understand* ... ?"

Tears were rolling down her cheeks, and she struggled to break away from him. "I don't *know* why you made me come here," she said huskily. "I wish I hadn't come. This will be Sonja Liczak's house. You should have brought her with you—"

"This will never be Sonja Liczak's house." He bent his head, and his arms slipped about her. "Katherine, you have been so foolish, and you have

167

made me so angry, but I can't go on punishing you any longer. *Katherine* . . ."

And then he kissed her, and she felt the world slipping away, while sunlight slanted brilliantly through the dusty mullioned window, and outside, in a bare, leafless rose bush, a blackbird started to sing.

CHAPTER TEN

AFTER what seemed a very long time, she lifted her head and looked at him, and her eyes were starry and very blue, but also completely incredulous.

"Then you aren't going to marry—" she began, but he interrupted her.

"No, my darling, I'm not going to marry her, so you don't need to talk about her any more. How could you ... how *could* you think," cupping her face with one hand, and looking down into her eyes, "that I would plan to marry her, after I had almost *told* you ... Katherine, don't you remember that morning at the Villa Albinhieri? I was very upset because you had run away from me the night before, and you were so plainly certain that I was ... what is the word? ... 'trifling' with you! But I intended to tell you then that I loved you—to ask you to marry me. You must have known; but you behaved so strangely, and that night, at the opera, you hardly looked at me."

"You didn't look at me," she whispered.

"Didn't I?" He smiled. "Well, perhaps I was a little offended because it seemed to me that you were doing your best to point out to me exactly how unwelcome my attentions were, as far as you were concerned. I had arranged the visit to the opera because I wanted you to see precisely what can happen when a member of my family appears in public—although we probably won't be seeing very much of that sort of reaction in the future. I thought it was only fair that you should know the sort of thing you might be exposed to if you became a Karanska. But then I began to think, watching you, that you had no intention of becoming a Karanska . . . that you simply didn't want to marry me, and when I had convinced myself of that I only wanted to hurt you. I didn't know what I was going to do with my own future, for I realized then that I couldn't face it without you!" He drew her to him, and she buried her face in his shoulder. "And then you ran away, and Natalia wept, and reproached me—and although I was not really listening to her I suddenly realized that she was saying you had been in love with me. I couldn't believe it, but then my godmother came to me, and she told me . . . she told me . . ."

His voice became unsteady, and he drew Kathy's face back into the open. "Oh, my darling, why did you listen to her?"

"She—she was fond of you, and she didn't want anything to hurt you. *I* don't want anything to hurt you either, and I thought she must be right. And she was so certain that you didn't—didn't love me . . ."

"Oh, no, she wasn't." He smiled again, as if in grudging admiration for his godmother's perspicacity. "She knew very well that I adored you, and so she has told me. But for a time she thought that I would forget you, and that it would be better for me to do so. And then, when you went back to England, and we were all so stunned . . ." He paused, as if the memory of it still had the power to hurt him. "Katherine, you must try to understand my godmother. She *is* fond of you, and she sees now that you will make the best wife in the world for me, but at one time she thought it was my desire to return to Tirhania, and replace my brother as king, and it

170

seemed to her that if I were going to do that it would be best for me to marry Sonja. She knows now that if I had wished to make such an attempt it would have been with you as my wife, not Sonja, but she also knows, because I have told her, that I have no intention of trying to seize power in Tirhania. One day, perhaps, when everything has been settled, we will go there, but the old days of monarchy are ended, and I would not try to revive them. Katherine, will you mind very much being the wife of a mere ex-prince, whose principal ambition is to lead the life of an 'English country gentleman'—perhaps to become a farmer?"

Her eyes were brilliantly blue. "Oh, Leonid, I—I can't imagine anything more wonderful!"

"But are you really sure?" His smile was suddenly teasing. "You haven't yet told me whether my godmother was right, after all. You haven't said—"

"Leonid darling, I love you better than anything in the world," she assured him anxiously. "I've loved you for ages. But I didn't know . . . I mean, although you kissed me, and at one time I did begin to think that you . . . that you rather liked me, I was certain that you couldn't—couldn't *love* anyone like me. And then, that morning, when you were talking to me in the library at the Villa Albinhieri, and Sonja Liczak arrived . . . Well, you didn't seem to want to go on talking to me any longer, and I thought that perhaps it was because the sight of her reminded you—"

"Reminded me of my duty?" Leonid shook his head at her. "My sweet little innocent, Sonja and I were never engaged, and although, as we're rather close to one another in age, our parents may at one time have planned that we should marry, I don't think that either of us ever seriously considered the possibility. And as to the conversation that was broken off when Sonja arrived, that was simply because I knew we should probably interrupted at any minute, and I decided that when I did ask you to marry me I would prefer it to be at a time when we would be unlikely to be disturbed."

"But you didn't bother about me again," she couldn't resist reminding him. "Not until late that night, anyway. And then you were furious with me!"

"I did bother about you, *chérie*—I thought about you all day," he confessed rather wryly. "But then I wondered whether it was right—fair—to ask you to marry me until you really understood what you might be taking on, and so, as I've told you, I arranged that visit to the opera in Genoa, so that you could see what can happen when my family appears in public . . . especially in a country like Italy. We may never get that sort of reception again, and I at least, intend to lead as normal a life as possible, but I wanted you to realize . . . You were wonderful, of course: calm and serene, and not at all frightened, and I was so proud of you!"

"And then I spoke to that reporter." Kathy closed her eyes, as if the memory of the solecism she had inadvertently committed were too much for her. "I'm so sorry . . . oh, Leonid darling, I'm so very, very sorry!"

"You didn't know, sweetheart. How could you? I went into the matter, and the man admitted that he did not tell you he was from the Press. But what hurt me so much was the fact that you told him I was going to marry Sonja. You were so certain . . . and after the things I had said to you!"

"I didn't think I was good enough," she whispered. "I know I'm not good enough! But I will try . . . Leonid, I'll do my best!"

She was not allowed to continue.

Ten minutes later, Leonid glanced at his watch, and through the window at the fading light, and suggested that they ought to be going.

"We have quite a long journey ahead of us, *chérie*, and I don't want you to be tired." They paused in the doorway of the house, and he looked down at her quizzically. "If you're not quite sure about the house we can come down to look at it again before we buy it."

"Oh, I *am* sure. I love it." She was almost breathless with enthusiasm. "Leonid, we will buy it, won't we?"

"Yes, of course we will." He smiled at her soothingly. "Even if I hated it myself, we would have it, because you like it so much."

The last of the February daylight soon disappeared, and they were travelling back to London by the light of the car's powerful headlamps, but Kathy found it oddly restful, and in any case she was floating in such an aura of happiness that everything around her seemed gilded with a kind of fairy-tale unreality. She and Leonid talked a good deal, for they had a great deal to talk about, but when silences fell she was happy to lean back and study as much of his profile as she could see in the half-light, or simply stare into the velvety darkness hanging over the countryside beyond the windows.

At last she remembered to ask about Natalia, and immediately felt guilty because she had not remembered before. "How is she?" she asked, rather hesitantly. "Was she . . . very offended when I left so suddenly?"

Swiftly, Leonid turned his head and smiled at her. "She was hysterical, and, as I told you, she immediately decided that it was all my fault. She told me that she had been meaning to talk to me about you." He smiled again. "She knew exactly how I felt about you, for she really has a great deal of sense, and she told me that I had deserved everything that was happening to me."

"Will she—do you think she'll be pleased?" asked Kathy shyly. "I mean, when—"

"When she hears that you are going to marry me? My darling, she told me before I left Italy that she wanted you for a sister-in-law, and that I had got to arrange it." He laughed softly. "I rather think she has something to tell you, too."

When they eventually reached London Kathy imagined that he would drive her straight back to her hostel for the night, but instead he turned in among the dazzling lights of the West End, and before she quite realized what he was intending to do he had brought the car to a halt outside one of the city's largest and most famous hotels.

She blinked in the strong light when he led her through the foyer, and into one of the luxurious lounges, but she blinked even more when a familiar voice sounded close beside her, and a slender, graceful vision in a white silk cocktail dress appeared in front of her. She gasped, and stood stock still.

"Natalia!"

"My dearest, dearest Kathy!" The slender vision hugged her enthusiastically, and kissed her on both cheeks. "You are going to marry Leonid, and everything is wonderful!"

"How . . . how do you know?"

"Why, he promised me that if everything was well he would bring you here, and we would all celebrate together!" She kissed Kathy again, and then embraced her brother-in-law. "It is so marvellous, and I . . . and I . . ." She paused a moment, her whole face alight. "And I—I have something wonderful to tell you, too!" From somewhere in the background a tall, masculine figure stepped forward, and Kathy recognized Colonel Zanin. "Karl and I are going to be married." She looked at the Colonel, and Kathy saw that there was a new poise about her, a new serenity. Instinctively, the other girl knew that Natalia would no longer dwell upon the imagined assassination of her former husband . . . no longer run away from life and from her fellow human beings. She smiled at her warmly. "I *am* glad," she said. "So very, very glad . . ."

"The wedding will be very soon," Natalia said happily. "In a week's time."

"The double wedding," Lenoid corrected her. "Don't you agree, *chérie*?"

Kathy's eyes assured him that she did agree.

A long time later, after dinner, Kathy and Leonid were alone together for a short time in one of the deserted lounges, and Leonid smiled whimsically.

"I have a fondness for London hotels," he remarked. "I met you, remember, in a London hotel."

"And you were rather cruel to me," she reminded him with a smile.

"If I was cruel it was simply because I already loved you . . . as I love you now, and as I always will love you, my beautiful blue-eyed Katherine." He took her hand, and kissed it. "As I always will love you, my sweet princess."

THE END

Your FREE gift includes
- *Anne Hampson* — Beyond the Sweet Waters
- *Anne Mather* — The Arrogant Duke
- *Violet Winspear* — Cap Flamingo
- *Nerina Hilliard* — Teachers Must Learn